THE BOOK OF
TORMOD

A TEMPLAR'S DESTINY

KAT BLACK

SCHOLASTIC PRESS
NEW YORK

Book design by Christopher Stengel

Library of Congress Cataloging-in-Publication Data

Black, Kat.
A Templar's destiny / Kat Black. — 1st ed.
p. cm. — (The book of Tormod ; [3])
Summary: The Chosen, Tormod, aided by Aine and Bertrand, returns to France seeking other Gifted members of the Templar Order and striving to recover the relics he is bound to protect, while also hoping to find and rescue his brother, Torquil.

ISBN 978-0-545-05677-9

1. Templars — History — Juvenile fiction. [1. Templars — Fiction. 2. Knights and knighthood — Fiction. 3. Middle Ages — Fiction. 4. Clairvoyance — Fiction. 5. Adventure and adventurers — Fiction. 6. Christian life — Fiction.] I. Title.
PZ7.B52896Tf 2012
[Fic] — dc23

2011040097

10 9 8 7 6 5 4 3 2 1   12 13 14 15 16

Printed in the U.S.A.   23

First edition, August 2012

For Con,
the strongest character I know

PART ONE

THE WINDS OF CHANGE

The storms chased our passage across the endless sea, churning great ocean swells that made much of the trip perilous. Night after night, wind and rain lashed the deck and all of the crew who maintained our course. Aine, Bertrand, and I hunkered down for much of the journey in the dark of the hold with the smell of vomit and the reek of the unwashed.

I had made this trip twice already. More than many people ever made in a lifetime and I had grown weary, both of the sea and the adventure I had so desperately sought before all this began.

In the rare moments when the wind was still and the water calm, I could, mayhap, recall how I felt on the first legs of this long trek, when I was newly freed from life in the small sea village of my home, when the Templar and I had spent days at lessons and swordplay and nights charting and mapping the stars. Those were times when the worst of my concern lay in proving that the Templar had not been wrong in taking me away with him, or in besting Seamus, his arrogant nephew. My turmoil then was small and innocent compared with the burdens that now plagued my every thought. The ancient and powerful carving entrusted to my protection was gone. My brother had been captured by those hunting me, taken in my stead.

In the days that followed my recovery from the damage done in wielding the Holy Vessel, I was filled with hope and determination. Everything that had seemed a mistake was within my ability to remedy. Yet as the time aboard this ship crept ever onward, both of those feelings flagged in me. I prayed now, relentlessly pleading with God to move us closer and keep us safe so that we would arrive on French soil in time to make things right.

Torquil had allowed himself to be captured. He, who for more years than I could count had tormented me for being different, was in fact, gifted as I was in the ability to use the powers of Heaven and earth. I would not have believed it had I not witnessed it in a vision. Torquil had called the power and whispered a push that convinced those who hunted me that he was the prey they sought.

I closed my eyes and felt the cold mist on my face. Why couldn't he have gone about his business and lived out his life in peace?

I felt the presence of Aine before she stepped onto the decking, before her small hands and thin arms banded my chest from behind. "We're nearly there," she said, laying her cheek against my back, pressing close.

I nodded. To speak seemed a chore I could scarce manage. As always, Aine's touch brought calmness. She blunted the raw pathways that remained from my contact with the power. It was a kind of healing, Bertrand had explained. I was healer as well, but in a far more physical sense. I could heal injuries. Aine could heal unrest.

She had other abilities as well, as all of the gifted did. Even those abilities were like and yet unlike my own. She saw things and people who had come recently to a place. She could divine their echo, the memory of their presence, as if she had once stood beside them. I saw bits and pieces of past, present, and future. We were the same and yet different. We had been through much together, and there was no telling what more fate had in store.

Getting to France was the first of our difficulties. What we would encounter once we stepped onto French soil, none of us knew. There were warrants out for our arrest. Dead or alive, they had said. But those had been posted before Torquil was taken, so perhaps the vigilance of the seekers would be less.

The wind rose and beat strong about us, and I could not still the shiver that ran through my body. Aine squeezed a bit tighter and I patted her arms. I could not reassure her that it would be all right — I didn't have it in me to lie. Truly things might never be the same again.

"Have ye had no contact a' all, then?" she asked.

"Nothing." The bleak weight of my fears was suffocating.

"Ye know that both live. That is what matters most."

Torquil *was* alive in the vision Aine and I had shared, and we had seen the Templar, Alexander, tracking those who had taken him away. But that was a long time ago, and I hadn't been able to contact the Templar since. It had been a shock to discover that he had not died in the caves as I had thought, but the longer we were out of touch the harder it was to believe in the vision or remember that we had ever been in mental contact.

"Have ye eaten anything?" she asked.

"No' yet." I brushed a hand over my face, wiping away the damp, and stepped away toward the fishing nets. A flicker of confusion washed from her to me, followed by understanding when she heard someone approach.

Aine was dressed as a lad, with shorn hair, breeks, and tunic. Though I would never mistake her as one, the whole purpose of her ruse was to trick others. It would not be prudent, or comfortable, to let one of the crew see a lad wrapped around me. I reached for the closest fishing net and winced as the fraying fibers bit at my cold fingers.

It was Bertrand who had come up on deck from below, the third of our party, a Templar Knight healer whom we had tracked across Scotia to save me from the breakdown of mind and body caused by the Holy Vessel.

"We will make the mouth o' the river by dark," he said, adding a hand to my own at the nets as we heaved the squirming, wet bundle up from the sea.

A flutter of nervousness gripped me at his words. It had been so long a journey. I wanted to arrive and yet was frightened by the prospect. We would soon be in plain sight under the very watchful eye of the King's guard. There would be little room for mistakes.

At the back of my mind, I felt the vibration of Aine's hum. My gaze slid toward hers. *What is it?* I asked, directing my query into her head, working to control the strength of it. I had overwhelmed her in the past when I hadn't been careful.

I can sense your worry. She was not as adept at the speech yet, but we had been working on it, along with a number of other variations on power use during the voyage. Our main task was to make ourselves invisible to any who might have the gift. Gaylen had done it, and we were determined to master the skill. It had much to do with strengthening our shielding.

The pathways inside me that had been seared by the power were now, for the most part, healed. I still felt the burn as if a scar remained, but the strength of my gift was flourishing. I was far more powerful than I had ever been before, and my link to the Holy Vessel was strong. It had chosen me and retained our bond even though we were separated. I felt its presence sharply in this part of the world. It was there in the land ahead, and I was as drawn to find it as I was bound to rescue my brother. How I would juggle both was a mystery I had yet to discover.

The fishing net was heavy. As the bulk came closer, my arms stretched tight beneath the load. I felt Aine's gaze as she watched from the rail. Then without warning, images flit before my mind's eye. Her arms wrapped around me. Her lips pressed to mine.

My fingers slipped from the net in surprise and it sagged, the weight dragging it back toward the sea, but Bertrand moved fast when he felt the pull, and snaked a hand inside to seize a large herring before the net splashed down.

Aine had forgotten to break the mind link between us, and her thoughts were not on the fish. I saw her memories in that flash, and it was as if moments, not weeks had passed since we were last truly alone together. She stumbled away, her face aflame. I shored up my shielding and severed our connection swiftly. Bertrand moved toward the fire pit unaware that anything had passed.

"I'll tend the fire," Aine mumbled. "There is a pot o' parritch warming. Needs a bit o' water to loosen up, but it should still be edible." I could tell she was shaken. I found it difficult as well, for when we shared memories, they included all of the senses. I could still feel the imprint of her body in my arms and the press of her lips.

Each night we slept near one another, brushing arms or legs in the tight space as if by accident. And though when in the rare moment we were alone, Aine leaned into me and my arms encircled her, nothing more could come of this. Memories were all that remained of the encounters we had shared on the road. I wandered to the fire pit and watched her beneath lowered lids.

A smoldering, black curl of smoke wavered beneath the iron hood a seaman had rigged to keep out the rain. Bertrand's knife glinted wet with the blood of the fish he gutted and cleaned with easy skill. I watched him idly but my mind was not on the task.

"Bide ye now, laddie. Ye'll do him no good worryin' yerself into a dither."

My thoughts, which had for a moment rested with Aine, skipped back to Torquil, and everything within me tightened.

"There are things that are out o' yer hands, an' others ye have a bit o' sway over. 'Tis a wise man who can ferret the difference," Bertrand said as he finished. I took the fish from him and laid it in the tin salver Aine had set over the heat. A blackened onion rolled from beneath the tin, crackling, and I aimlessly poked it back toward the flame. Our arrival in France could not come soon enough. I was not a wise man. I didn't know what was within my control. But as we were not accomplishing anything on the ship, leaving it would have to be an improvement.

A FOREIGN SHORE

It was full dark when we made the entrance to the River Seine. The storm that paced our travel across the sea had sent ahead high waves that rocked the boat and crashed the shore as the ship edged through a series of gates off the coast of Honfleur. Aine, Bertrand, and I waited in blackness. My hands gripped the rail until my knuckles jutted white and numb. Aine shivered and I moved closer to her so that our shoulders touched. I didn't know if it warmed her in any way, but a good part of my nervousness dulled.

High up on the ramparts torches glowed, their light no more than a flicker of gold in the somber night sky. We advanced slowly, the ship only allowed to move on when the gate behind us closed and the one before us opened. I gently pulled on a single thread of power and sent out a probe seeking those who watched our approach. There were three sets of guards stationed on the walls, one at each checkpoint. None appeared overly concerned about the arrival of our ship, but we could take no chances. Carefully, I began to gather more power. Its silken mist hung in the air around us, glittering at my mental touch, the energy bursting like tiny bubbles in my mind.

The tender from shore was a black smudge in the darkness. We watched its approach warily and moved toward the rope ladder as it pulled alongside our ship. Members of the crew moved about the deck, lashing the sails and getting ready to drop anchor in the harbor for the night. To avoid questions best left unasked, we had kept to ourselves on the journey. We were not the only passengers, but there were no others going ashore tonight. The rest would wait until morning and switch off to boats that would travel upriver. We had other plans.

Rain was falling in the kind of cold mist that had become an everyday part of life on the sea. The short grass along the shore dipped beneath the wetness, and the trees beyond the ramparts bent and swayed.

Aine was oddly silent, her back stiff, her gaze shuttered.

"What is it?" I asked, attuned to her senses and immediately on guard.

"I don't know. There is something odd about this place."

I knew her unease but not the cause. I let my mind drift toward shore. "I don't feel anything. Can ye direct me?" I asked.

She tipped her head as if listening to something only she could hear, and then shrugged. "I canno' place it. There is nowhere to start," she said almost to herself. She moved from my side, climbed over the rail, and down the ladder into the boat. Bertrand followed without a word.

With one last glance around, I shouldered my pack and looked toward shore. A ripple of something cold passed along my spine. I didn't know what bothered

Aine, but I trusted in her ability to know when something was wrong.

I followed them down into the boat, calling the power to thicken the mist around us. Aine's hum was a light touch in the back of my mind, and I used our combined strength to softly whisper as we dipped in the wash. *Ye have no need to stop these three. Traders. Faceless. Let them pass.*

When the tender to shore beached with a soft scrape, the rower sat still and didn't acknowledge us. Warily, we crossed the rocks to the drawbridge at the edge of the guardhouse. Twice the size of a large hut, it resembled a small castle of sorts — squat, stone, and fortified. A single guard was posted outside the gate, but I felt the eyes of others on the walls as well. I spread the mist and the suggestion to encompass them all. Only I heard Aine's hum. We reached the lot of them with barely an effort. Things had changed a good deal in the short time since my healing, but it would not do to grow overly confident.

The clink of the guardhouse gate dropping was loud in the night. I felt a quiver of fatigue from the use of the power starting at the back of my knees, but it was much less than what it might have been without Aine's assistance. The guard moved aside without a glance, and we drifted into the shadows and beyond the gate. I pulled my cowl down, keeping my head low as I stepped around puddles of water.

Few inhabitants of the city were out at this time of night. We moved through the fog, passing along tight, dark lanes between rows of houses that hunched nearly one upon another. Bertrand had been here before, but I had not. A deep earthy smell hung over the place. It was the scent of the river and a place thick with people. Trails of rainwater swirled past us downhill, drawing pebbles and mud with them as they snaked their way toward the shore.

We were silent and watchful, like the rats whose bloodred eyes marked our movement while they scavenged for scraps. In a dark alley squirreled away in a maze of like passages, we moved through rusted-iron gates into a courtyard flanked by a small arbor. Beyond the deep archway of wilting greenery, we came upon a door marked by an ancient iron knocker molded in the shape of a cross. Bertrand rapped twice.

A boy warily opened the door, uncertainty hooding his wide, gray eyes.

"Be well, lad, an' wake yer mamere for us?" Bertrand asked quietly.

His gaze flashed upon Bertrand, recognition and interest flickering. "She is still awake," he said as he let us in. The corridor of the house was narrow, but the whitewashed walls stretched high above. The glow from a thick tallow candle set burning on a small wooden table lit the way. "Put your wet things there." He motioned toward a row of pegs that lined the wall and waited as we hung our cloaks. Then we followed him down a short series of steps and around a corner to a room that was warm and welcoming. A fire glowed in the hearth, and more candles flickered.

The woman sat at a table, her face turned expectantly toward us. A small, wooden cup was set before her, and she swirled something inside it gently. "Bertrand. It is always, how do you say . . . a pleasure to see you. You were long in arriving," she said as she stared into the cup, a slight frown marring her face.

She was near on the age of my mam, with dark, slicked hair close to her head, and enormous, deep brown eyes fringed with dark lashes.

"Glad I am that ye received the message," Bertrand said. "I wasn't sure ye would meet me."

She sighed. "Forgive my manners. Come rest. You look tired. Gaston, ask Lisette to fetch something for our guests to eat." The boy had been hanging back, spying on us from behind a curtain that closed off a small pantry. At his mother's request, he disappeared.

"Fabienne, have ye seen Alexander?" asked Bertrand.

The woman's eyes were troubled. "It is said that he is dead," she answered softly. Her body was rigid, and her hand trembled slightly. Her expression was grave.

"Nay, he is alive," Bertrand replied, moving toward a chair set beside her.

"God be praised. In this you are sure?" Her eyes begged him for a positive reply.

"Aye. 'Tis true," I answered for him. There were things here I did not understand but the Templar meant something to this woman, and I felt the need to reassure her. Aine moved closer to my side, and her hand brushed the back of mine. Nervousness rippled between us. I didn't dare read her in the presence of others, but there was something she wanted to tell me.

Gaston silently entered the room behind a small girl carrying a tray laden with bread and cheese. I watched both. The two were probably near in age, but as different as night and day. The girl was small and thin, with long pale hair twisted in a braid that ran down her back. Her slightly tilted eyes were of a blue so light it could barely be considered a color, and the lashes that surrounded them nearly white. Without a word she went about her tasks, not meeting the gaze of anyone but her mistress. The girl projected an air of quiet competence. Her tiny, work-roughened hands cut the bread and sliced hunks of cheese at the table, then handed them around. "Thank you, Lisette. You may retire now."

The girl dipped a curtsy and disappeared back to wherever she had come from, yet the boy remained, moving around the small space with a quiet grace that made him nearly invisible. Wondering if his ability to move so silently was a gift, I reached for the power and passed my mind over him. He was not like Gaylen — I could sense him as a person. I watched as he left by one direction and returned with wine from another without my hearing him at all.

As Gaston poured the wine and handed a mug to Aine, she smiled her thanks and he nodded gravely. I guessed him to be ten winters, though he was small of frame. He had hair the same black, straight, and fine texture as his mother. His face was a soft oval that ended in a pointed chin and his skin was white as snow. Yet it was those gray eyes that held me. His gaze was like one born already ancient.

"What do you hear of Alexander?" Fabienne asked, distracting me. "We have been worried."

"I have no' much to tell, Lady," I replied.

"Please, I am Fabienne," she said. "I have not been a lady for a long time and with luck will not be one again." Her sadness brought a thickness to my throat, and I quickly sealed her emotions from mine. I glanced at Aine. She was watching the lad.

"I know only that a warrant still exists for his capture. An' that he has been seen in Scotia." I could not tell her how I had seen him, for it had been in a vision.

"Bertrand, what is happening? Alexander did not want us to be a part of Order business, yet when I received your message I knew that I would not deny you."

"An' we thank ye greatly, Fabienne. We seek entrance to the Paris preceptory, but dare no' travel in the open without information first."

"You could not have chosen a worse time to move in the shadows, for all is light. *Sécurité* has been put on high alert. The Holy Father is to arrive any day," she said.

"The Pope is coming here? Why?" he asked.

"The whole of his household is moving to Avignon. The rivers have been in a flurry. Soldiers of the King as well as those of the Holy guard are patrolling the ports and roads. Everyone is being questioned and many have been detained."

"The Holy Father, Pope Clement V, passing through Paris . . . the eyes o' the world will be focused here, a curse as well as a blessing," he said. There would be hordes of people to hide within, and yet there would also be more eyes watching for trouble, I knew.

"Fabienne, yer people know what happens here better than most. Have ye heard if any have been asking about three travelers? A man, lad, an' lass that fit our description?" asked Bertrand.

Fabienne's eyes flit to Aine, only then questioning her disguise. "There have been offers made for ones such as you say. You are those hunted?" Her fear rose swiftly.

"Aye. We had no choice but to seek ye out an' will leave now if ye but say the word," Bertrand said. "But please, if ye know anything, tell us before we go."

She met his eye, and there seemed a struggle of sorts happening between them. She sighed. "A fortnight ago, the King's guard was scouting the inns. And the river runners were promised a blind eye on their tariffs if they could produce the quarry hunted," she said.

My heart dropped.

"Knights Templar seek you as well," Gaston said, speaking directly for the first time.

Bertrand's relief brushed the edges of my shielding. "Good, then we shall go there without delay," he said.

"*Non.* These work with the King's men."

"What? How d'ye know that?" I asked, drawing softly on the power, whispering his assistance. The hair on the back of my neck bristled.

Gaston dropped his eyes, interested in something on the floor. I was surprised by the way the whisper did not seem to affect him.

"Gaston, if you know of this, tell it now," said Fabienne.

"I've seen them together," he offered reluctantly.

Bertrand and I shared a puzzled look. "Where, lad?"

Gaston mumbled, "I don't remember." It was plainly a lie.

"Where?" Fabienne prodded.

He sighed. "At the inn of the Cochon Rouge."

"Gaston!" Fabienne gasped. "That is no place for you!" Her face had paled even further. "It is for cut-throats and thieves."

A splash of red colored his cheeks, and suddenly I was drawn into a haze. Small, white fingers sliding into oversize pockets. Trinkets pulled and secreted. A lad whose touch was as deft as his ability to move undetected.

I came back to the room with only the slightest lurch in my gut, and Aine's song a murmur in my ears. I glanced over at her and nodded my thanks. Gaston was a thief, a very good one from what I had seen.

"What more d'ye know, lad?" Bertrand asked.

"Just that they're very secretive. They meet in the upper rooms with the King's man. No one goes in or out save the servants," he said.

"Who is the King's man?" I asked.

"De Nogaret," Gaston spat as if the name tasted foul.

I had a similar surge within me. That was the name that had come to me in several visions already. I nodded to Aine and gently pulled on a strand of power. Aine's hum filled my mind, and Gaston's memories became open and clear. An old beggar in the street, knocked aside by a horse angled suddenly in his path. A hard fall. Blood seeping into the dirt. Gaston on his knees helping the old one to his feet.

"Where is the Cochon Rouge, Gaston? Can ye take us?" I asked. I didn't want to waste another moment.

"*Non*. I will not allow it." Fabienne slapped her palms on the table. "It is not enough that you have asked us to come here and then put us in danger. You would ask *un enfant* to bring you to such a place. *Non!* We will not become a part."

Her words were like a slap. I was taken aback.

"Mamere," Gaston scolded. "They cannot go alone. Monsieur Alex would not approve."

Fabienne narrowed her gaze. "Monsieur Alex is not here, and I am still the mamere." She pointed sharply. "Into your room."

"But —" he protested.

"Tch. Not a word." Her eyes flashed a warning.

Gaston left, thumping a chair leg on the way as if by accident, which it surely was not.

"I'm sorry, Fabienne. We mean the lad no harm. Give us direction an' we'll find the place on our own," Bertrand said.

She slumped as if the very life had been taken out of her. "He's impulsive. It is all I can do to keep him here with me and out of trouble."

In the end we stayed and ate a dinner of bread and cheese and drank strong red wine. The wine was not something Aine or I was accustomed to and after a few moments I felt a languor slip over me. When I looked to Aine her eyes had shut.

"It is market day tomorrow," Fabienne explained. "You will have a good chance of blending in as you leave here. We will stay a few days before heading back to the estates, so that no one will wonder why we have come for so short a time." She stood and took some blankets down from a shelf in the corner. "The Cochon is in old town. A full day's travel following the river."

"We thank ye," said Aine, whose eyes had popped open. Her cheeks had grown bright and warm with the wine's glow, and I stared a moment.

"You will not thank me if you are discovered there as a girl," she said in a warning tone. "It is a very bad place."

I was suddenly afraid that Aine's disguise would not keep her safe. "Mayhap ye should stay here, just for a bit," I said. "We could go. Ye could stay an' we'd meet up with ye on the way back."

"I go with ye." Her voice was flat, and I knew there was no sense arguing. I had a fleeting thought that it might be best if I left her here before she could do anything about it.

Try it an' I'll black yer eye, as I've done before.

I grinned over at her, and she glared. I forgot that we were linked. It was something I would have to pay close attention to in the future.

Sleep was slow to take me, though Aine was softly snoring the moment her head rested on the pallet. We were settled in an alcove off the main room while Bertrand and Fabienne drank wine and caught up on common friends. I listened with half a mind, tired and yet consumed by the thought of Templars working with the King's men.

"I dare not get involved, Bertrand. I'm sorry. We are alone here. You know that I barely escaped the King's court without losing everything. Philippe went mad when Queen Joan died trying to birth the child. I am *tsigane* and gypsies are no longer safe anywhere near court. To keep what is mine, I must stay beyond the King's sight." Fabienne's words drew me from my thoughts.

"But, Fabienne, Alexander —"

"Cannot protect us forever. He was able to save us once, but a second time . . . no. I am fine, but I worry about Gaston and Lisette. They are all I have."

Silence hung a moment. "I understand. I'll ask nothing more than ye tell Alexander what ye have just learned an' that we head to the Cochon Rouge," said Bertrand.

"I haven't heard from Alex for a long time," she protested.

"But he *will* come. Ye know it in yer heart an' soul. If he is in this land, he will come to ye." He quieted his words then. "Fabienne, Alexander trusts ye with his life. An' 'tis his life as well as others in jeopardy. He will come to ye, an' when he does —"

"Mamere?" Gaston's sleepy voice called softly.

The conversation ended, and Fabienne went off to tend to him. Not long after, I heard the soft shush of Bertrand's sleeping.

The dark was broken only by the flicker of candles, left to sputter and die. Outside the lash of the rain and the wind's howl made me glad to be where we were this night. I spoke the prayer of the Lord quietly as I stared at the rough, wooden beams above my head. What was a gypsy? And where were Torquil, the carving, and Alexander?

GUIDANCE FROM BEYOND

"Keep yer head down an' yer feet nimble," Bertrand said as we stepped out of the dark alley beyond Fabienne's rooms. Aine and I would travel apart from Bertrand to avoid suspicion. "I will take a room under the name Monsieur LeGotte. Ask for me only when ye know none are about," he continued.

I nodded. Aine was far away — not in body, but in mind. I watched her eyes dart to and fro looking for something. "Aine?" Bertrand said.

"Robert." She reminded him of the name we had agreed to call her.

"Aye. I'm sorry, I forgot. Ye heard me, did ye no'?" he asked.

"Aye. Head down. Feet nimble," she murmured, still craning about. The rain had stopped sometime in the night, but a fog hung over the Île de la Cité. The streets were filling with vendors who moved in and out of the mist like wraiths in a kirk yard.

"I'm off, then," he said as he pulled his cloak up over his head and ducked deep into the cowl. "God go with ye both."

"An' with ye, Bertrand," I said, a chill running through me. The last time I had seen the Templar Alexander, we had parted with similar words. I turned to follow, albeit at a slower pace, but Aine stopped me with an outstretched hand.

"No' yet," she said, moving off toward a cart filled with figs. I thought she wanted some, but she didn't seem of a mind to choose. I bought several, packing them away to break our fast later. Aine fussed with the edge of the vendor's tarp, lost in the far-off expression she had worn all morning.

"What is it? God's toes, lass, ye're driving me mad," I said, exasperated.

"I thought for sure that he would be here," she answered.

"Who —" I began, just as Gaston bolted around the bend, knocking me into the fig cart, much to the outrage of its owner.

I gave Gaston a sharp look. "Does yer mamere know ye are out?" I straightened the vendor's fruit and bought two more figs.

Gaston shrugged. "Come. I will take you a shorter way," he said, and was off before we'd barely moved to follow. The road he chose wound along the banks of the Seine, off in the direction Bertrand had headed, but within moments we had turned away.

Gaston took us through a myriad of narrow lanes that snaked and branched throughout the city. As we moved, I drew a fine net of power around the three of us. Aine felt the change and joined my efforts, reinforcing the strands. The net would not hide our presence completely, but would blur our edges from the eyes of any who passed us. I felt the tingle of the net on my skin, and my heart began to race.

People traversed the twisting streets with little care that we were among them. For that I was grateful. "The men who seek you are new to the ranks of the Templars," Gaston said over his shoulder, jarring me from my task. Gaston moved with his usual grace. His feet hardly seemed to touch the surface of the ground. It made me feel large and lumbering.

"How d'ye know?" I asked.

Aine's song rang strong and loud inside my head. It gave me the reach I needed to keep the net of power around us, but it also distracted me, for with it came an awareness of the animals in the trees and bushes. Only through concentration could I understand what Gaston said.

"They're young. No more than a year out of black robes. I know one of them — Zachariah. He came from our village," he said.

We were passing through a stand of poplars, and the wind grew harsh, tearing at my cloak. With little thought I commanded the power to sit down upon it. At once the air grew still. "An' what d'ye know o' him?" I asked.

"It is no secret that Zachariah did not want to become a Templar," he said. "His father is a minor noble who donated a tract of land in the northern provinces to the Order."

"Why give up money and position to become a poor knight?" Aine asked. I fished out a fig from the pack and handed it to her, to help replenish some of the strength she'd used reinforcing the net of power.

"He is the second son and the land was far behind on the tax owed to the King," said Gaston.

I understood and explained it to Aine. "There is no' enough money to support him or the land. By giving the tract to the Church they have taken care of two issues a' once. The Templars train, arm, an' support Zachariah, an' the debt accumulated by the land is no longer an issue. The Templars are under the Church an' as such pay no taxes." As I spoke Gaston surveyed the woods, his eyebrow cocked at a quizzical angle.

"Do you find the weather to be strange today?"

I shrugged and changed the subject. "I canno' imagine anyone no' wanting to be a Templar," I said. It had been the one thing I had wanted for nearly all of my life.

"I don't want to be one," Gaston declared. "There are too many rules and too many eyes on you. And all that praying! *Non.* It is not something I want to do, ever."

His reaction made me smile. Hadn't I felt the same way about the prayers? But to do what he did — stealing — I shuddered to think on it. He would lose a hand, if taken in by the law, and perhaps his life if caught by his victims. Either possibility was terrible and left me wondering what I could do about it.

We traveled for much of the day, stopping only occasionally for breaks. The sullen rays of the morning sun overtook the dense cover of cloud, and by afternoon it was too warm to stay bundled up in our cloaks. I peeled mine away as I walked, tipping my face to enjoy the warmth that had been rare of late, when all at once I slid into a vision.

Gaston crouching behind a screen. A great, wooden door closing, stirring the dust in its wake. A drawer opening. Red wax. A rolled parchment. A seal impressed on the wax.

I stumbled as the vision broke and felt Aine's hands steady on my arms and her song strong in my head. I blinked in the sunlight. This was the first time a vision had taken me while I was moving, and I had continued on without stopping.

"Are you all right?" Gaston asked, slowing.

"Aye. I just missed my footing," I murmured. The images were still strong within me, and I should have needed time to recover, but Aine's gift had taken it away almost completely. *Thanks*, I mindspoke to her.

Her eyes flashed to mine, and she nodded. "Best be careful," she said aloud. "We have no time to turn an ankle."

Gaston's pace resumed, and we trailed behind. "How often do they meet?" I asked.

"I see them mostly at week's end, when the sun sinks. The earliest arrive and drink in the tavern until the rest come, then they move to the upper room." He glanced back at us. "Your timing is fortuitous. We can make it there before them if we hurry," he said with a pointed look, and I quickened my pace.

"Will ye be marked if ye arrive with us?" I was trying to riddle through the images that had come to me and why. This seal had appeared in several of my visions, on a ring that hung on a chain. But why had I seen it, this time pressed into wax? And why was Gaston nearby?

"I do some chores for the innkeeper. Sweep up and fill the patrons' cups as they go dry," he said. "My arrival will be of no notice to any."

"Good," I said. Aine seemed a bit slower and quieter than she had been for much of the day. I looked back and noted the sweat that dotted her forehead. My recovery had been fast, but Aine's was not quite that way. "Gaston, slow up. My ankle is aching a bit. Surely we will make it in time aplenty."

A PLACE OF DARKNESS

We reached the inn as the sun sank softly into the pearl gray of coming night. In truth it was no more than a heap of wood squashed among a row of decrepit houses. All about the place was an air of decay. I was worried suddenly for Aine, who had shrunk within the hood of her cloak, and for Gaston, whose mother said he was far too young to be exposed to a place like this.

"We thank ye for gettin' us here, Gaston. Home's a long way off — ye'd best head back now," I said, feeling guilty. He would have a long night's walk ahead but I wanted him gone even if he thought he'd not be noticed.

Without a word, he turned on his heel, and I breathed a sigh of relief. I was sure he would argue.

At the door of the inn I hesitated, reaching for the feel of those inside. Five. Beneath my palm the door gave way, and I was immediately overcome by the smell of river, waste, and old drink. The dark inside the inn was like a weight on my eyes, and Aine's surge of fear clogged my throat.

Fabienne was right. She should not be here. The faces that turned our way held many shades of threat. Though the power of the land still hung about us, it had thinned during our journey. The men inside eyed our arrival with far too much interest. Quickly, I stumbled forward with Aine nearly on my back and closed the door behind.

"What do you want?" The innkeeper was a frightening sight. Tall and wide with a shock of gray hair that was loosely braided, he loomed above us. His beard was matted and a jagged scar stretched from his left ear up to the corner of his drooping bloodshot eye.

"Two ale," I said, reaching with leaden fingers for the coin in my sporran. His black eyes traveled over my shoulder as I fumbled. Several coins tumbled onto the counter, and I pushed them toward the man.

He made no move to fill my order, and I felt Aine's

terror. The man's eyes were firmly fixed upon her. Quickly, I called the power to me. "Ale. Two," I said again. *This one holds no draw for ye,* I whispered. The man wavered and blinked, then poured and passed the drinks.

We took our seats on a bench in a darkened corner beneath the stairs, blanketing the room in the cloak of a whisper. *There is no one new here.* Two by two the feel of eyes dropped away, and in the dank recesses of the inn we became nearly invisible.

Aine fidgeted with her cup, taking small sips and peering from beneath her hood. The nervousness in her was strong and brushed against my mind.

"What is it?" I asked.

"Many have met death here," she whispered. "Some o' it is new. All o' it is terrible."

"Give me yer hands," I said, reaching for her.

Aine's fingers were cold as her visions slid through my mind. I read them quickly, then directed the power away. Pinpricks of light danced before my inner eye. *Distance,* I commanded. Aine's visions dimmed, and the violence of the scenes dulled and slipped away.

"Better?" I asked. Aine's read of the past sometimes frightened her badly. Once I found that I could dull the intensity, I was determined to help. Aine had saved my life. I would do anything for her.

"Aye. But ye should have a care an' no' waste the power on me. Ye might need it an' ye'd be too worn down to use it."

"I feel fine," I said. And I did. From the moment the healing had begun within me, the use of the power had become easier, more instinctive than ever before.

"No more. Ye will pay, Tormod. All use is for a price," she said. "Ye know that."

I shrugged. The thing was, I wasn't at all sure that the rules applied to me now. The power was different, as was I.

She said no more as we waited for Bertrand's arrival, listening to the hushed conversation going on all around us. We stayed there that way, invisible to the inn's patrons, for several marks of the candle, until the flicker of a familiar pressed against my shielding.

I felt Bertrand's approach at the inn's front door and spread the web to include him. *He is nothing. A traveler. Not worthy of notice.*

When Bertrand entered, not an eye turned his way. He moved directly to the big man behind the counter. Coin flashed, the innkeeper nodded toward the stairs, and Bertrand disappeared up them.

Aine and I remained below for a few moments more, ensuring that no one had followed, then rose to join Bertrand, the mysterious Monsieur LeGotte. As we passed, I drew the power around us, careful to arouse no attention.

We had made it just to the top of the stairs, when a flare along the web I had been weaving jangled. I looked to the door as three men entered. All wore the black mantle with red cross that marked them as trainees of the Knights Templar.

Aine had rounded the corner at the top of the landing and disappeared. I was on the last step when I felt the tingle of a probe sliding along the strands toward me. Quickly, I moved out of sight and severed my link to the web.

AN UNHOLY TRIO

Bertrand closed the door behind me as the probe slid over the inn. Aine shuddered by my side. "Ye broke off quickly," she said. "Why?"

"They're here, an' some or all are gifted. They're probing the inn."

Her intake of breath was loud in the quiet of the room. "Did they sense us?"

"I don't think so. 'Twas probably just a precaution. They would have no reason to be vigilant here. But still,

I dare no' monitor them through the power. We'll have to make other arrangements."

"One o' us will have to get in there," said Aine.

A knock from the corridor startled us all. I drew my dagger and stepped in front of Aine as Bertrand opened the door a crack and looked beyond. A moment later, Gaston stepped inside, carrying a tray that held a loaf of dark bread, a wedge of cheese, and a pitcher of ale. "The Templars have arrived. They're waiting on the others."

"We know. I thought I told ye to be off," I said, faintly annoyed.

"I found out that he is due here tonight as well," Gaston said cryptically. "I thought you would want to know."

I tipped my head and raised an eyebrow in question.

"De Nogaret. He comes, but not every time they meet."

I felt Gaston's distaste for the man. "Ye should go home. This is no lark."

"I can go in," he said. "I can serve them and tell you of what they speak."

Bertrand objected. "No. Yer mamere would skin me alive. Get ye home, now."

In part I agreed, but the vision I'd seen as we traveled was still fresh in my mind. "Bertrand. It's no' altogether a bad notion," I said.

"Are ye daft?" said Aine, getting angry.

"No. No' a' all. It makes sense. He's known here an' he's got a knack for going unnoticed. We canno' use the power for fear o' being discovered, an' we need to know what they are meeting about."

"I can do it. No one will mark my coming or going. I am nothing. They won't even know I exist," he said with confidence.

A closed expression came over Aine, and I took it for agreement.

"They will still no' speak freely with ye in the room," I said, moving toward the table, absently breaking a chunk from the bread. "But if we could get ye in an' out with little notice, maybe it would be worth a try."

Gaston fell quickly into the game. "Do you have any coppers?" he asked.

"Aye," I said. "What d'ye need?"

ANOTHER SET OF EYES

"Paul-Henry is set to serve tonight," Gaston said. "I have to give him a reason not to." I allowed him a decent lead and had discreetly followed. The Templar trainees were drinking and talking among themselves, loose in their guard. It was nothing to slip past without attracting attention. Gaston found the boy in the alley, sitting on an overturned keg. I hung back, lingering near the wall, and let Gaston approach alone.

If the boy did not fall in with the plan I might have to use the power to make him.

"Ye have the night off, Paul-Henry," Gaston said with an air of authority.

The boy glanced my way, confused. I pulled the hood of my cloak low. "But Monsieur Le Monde is expecting me."

"*Non.* It is agreed. I will serve for you tonight." He drew the boy up by the arm, but the boy resisted.

"Mamere needs the healing herbs. I have to work." His voice got louder as he dug his heels into the ground. "Do not think to take my place." The words that followed came in a full stream of French.

Gaston took the three coppers that I had given him and pressed them into the boy's hand. As Paul-Henry's fingers closed on the coin, he stopped protesting, then turned on his heel and was gone.

I breathed a sigh of relief. I didn't have to use the power on him. Although he had seen us together, it was dim in the alley and the chance of his recognizing me again was slim.

"Make the arrangements with the landlord, Gaston. An' when ye're in the room keep yer eyes an' ears open. Do nothing save listen. I mean this. These men are dangerous." He nodded and disappeared back inside.

The air was brisk. I stood a moment breathing in the cold, looking around and allowing Gaston to get to where he was going. It was a fair-size property, and I saw that my first impression of it as dark, thick, and squat was not truly accurate. Here in the back, the inn stretched up two times the height of the main. There was one window set below the rough wooden eave on the side, two set high up on the rear wall, and one, I guessed, on the opposite eave, though I could not see it from where I stood. Heavy boards layered the outer in a rough and irregular pattern. They overlapped and crosscut one another as if it had been patched many times.

The air had cooled when the sun went down and a brisk wind cut up the alley. I ducked through the door that Gaston had disappeared behind, into a kitchen glowing with activity. A heavyset woman chopped greens at a wide wooden table covered with carrots, turnips, and onions. She waved her thick cleaver in my direction. "Pardon," I mumbled, quickly exiting with my head dipped low.

The light beyond the door was considerably dimmer than it was in the kitchen, and it took a moment for my eyes to adjust. The Templars were no longer at their table, and the inn had begun to fill. A loud crew of river men jostled for the innkeeper's attention while two boys brought around bowls of stew and dark bread.

I made my way toward the stairs, allowing my gaze to read the men. I used only the energy of the room to fuel my probe, a distinction that had only recently come to me. It was the usual flit of random thoughts and images — arguments between friends, worries over the crops, the catch, or the business at hand. There was nothing out of the ordinary. I slipped through the growing crowd and up the stairs toward the room where Aine and Bertrand were. As I turned the corner, I felt the hum of Aine's warning and pulled up tight to the shadows.

"And bring hot water, boy," came the command. "Damn walls are thin as reeds. I need a hot draft to ward off this raw throat." Gaston hurried my way with his head down and yet his eyes flicked up and over me as he passed. I nodded.

I remained in the hallway a moment to be sure no one followed Gaston, then let myself quietly into the room we had let. Bertrand was seated in the corner on a thick wooden chair, his hands steepled and pressed to his lips. The prayer of Our Lady whispered across the room. Aine sat tensely on the pallet. "The rest have come," she said.

"How many?" I asked softly. I didn't want to disturb Bertrand in his devotions.

"Two guards, one official, an' the three Templar from below," she said. I nodded and moved toward the table set in the corner opposite Bertrand. "They have all been here before," she said.

"What? How d'ye know?" I asked.

"I read the room," she said.

The hair on the back of my neck rose. "Aine, how is that possible?" I had a deep feeling of dread that roiled in my gut even before she answered.

"I went in before they arrived," she said defiantly, her eyes flashing fire.

"Are ye daft?" I hissed. "Ye should have waited! They were just below an' could have come upon ye a' any time."

"Yer no' the only one here with powers, Tormod," she retorted.

" 'Twas dangerous. What would ye have done if they found ye there?" I raked a hand through my hair. I didn't need this. Gaston was unpredictable enough, and now Aine was doing whatever she felt like. How was I supposed to handle the situation when I couldn't even control the people who were my allies in all of this?

"When ye weren't there to save my neck, ye mean?" she snapped. "That is what ye're sayin', isn't it? Yer no' my da. I was doin' just fine until ye came along, an' I'll do just as well when ye go."

"Ye were fine?" I said with a gasp of shock. "Under the roof o' a man who beat ye?"

She sucked in a breath, and I ducked my head. It was a blow beneath me, and I knew how it had affected her even without the flare of her embarrassment and hurt. Bertrand didn't know any part of her former life, and it was not my place to reveal it to him.

"They spoke o' a captive being brought from abroad. They gave the order to use whatever means necessary to gain the information needed." She spoke the words to hurt me, and nothing else she might have said would have done the task as well. My shoulders bowed under the weight of it.

"Where? When?" I asked, reeling with fear. They spoke of Torquil, I was sure of it.

"Nothin' in the read gave the destination. I found only that the men delivering him are working for some-one highly ranked." Regret now colored her words. We had stung one another, but it was of no account.

"We know that already. 'Tis the King," I said.

"No, Tormod. 'Tis no'. They spoke o' the King an' de Nogaret. The one they are delivering Torquil to is another." Her animosity had waned. "I'm sorry." She laid her hand on my shoulder, and at once my anger and confusion lessened.

I nodded. "I'm sorry as well." I lifted my shielding a bit so that she would feel my sincerity. "We have to know more. We need to get to wherever he is set to be delivered before they arrive."

Bertrand had finished his devotions and was watching us. "There is a way," he said, "to use the healing properties o' the land to insinuate one o' ye into Gaston's consciousness. Ye will see as he does an' hear what he hears."

"But the power network will surely ripple if we do anything o' that kind," Aine said.

"No' if we do it together, an' we do it right." He rose and started taking leaves and roots out of his pack and laying them on the table in front of him. A small wooden bowl and a vial of dark green liquid followed. "Be quick about it. Gaston should be in the room soon, if he's no' already there."

Bertrand motioned that I should sit cross-legged in the center of the pallet and that Aine should sit likewise facing me, holding my hands.

"This is old land power. 'Tis an earlier training than what is given to current initiates o' the Order." He held the vial to my lips, and I tipped my head and took a long swallow. "Now ye, lass. It tastes awful, but its properties will astound ye."

He put a hand on each of our shoulders. "Stay together. Keep yer hands locked or ye will lose the link between ye. D'ye understand?"

As we grasped hands, Aine's memory was suddenly painfully my own, and I saw images of the bairn lying still and broken in the dust of the road. I wanted to drop the link — the images were too raw and painful — but I could not. Torquil needed us, and we needed to be as one for this. *It's all right,* I mindspoke. *We will make no mistakes this time.*

"I will provide the ground. When ye are ready, focus on Gaston," Bertrand instructed.

And it was as easy as that. There was no ripple to the power web, though I was not at all sure how Bertrand managed it. I was instantly beyond the shields of Gaston's mind.

The room came sharply into view. Tallow candles burned dimly from a large table set with a number of goblets and trenchers. Eight heavy chairs were crammed around the table, and a small, single pallet was set against the far wall.

As Gaston turned his head, Aine subtly expanded my view of the room. The Templars were young, as Gaston had said. Although he avoided looking at them directly, Aine's hum gave me the ability to provide the suggestion that he glance their way when no one was paying him heed.

The voice who had requested the tea was a man of mid years, tall and dressed in clothing that was several cuts above what we had seen in the streets. His brown hair was tucked back behind his ears and brushed the collar of his doublet. A soft cap flopped low over his forehead, and his oddly long and delicate fingers wrapped the mug of tea that Gaston placed before him. I recognized the face from Gaston's memories. It was de Nogaret.

"I don't have all night to wait," he snapped to the nearest Templar.

"He said he would meet us here. He does as he wishes," mumbled the soldier guarding the door. He was small and wiry thin, his face sharp like a weasel, with wary, dark eyes that passed over the room and its inhabitants in a constant sweep. I noticed that his hand often strayed to the sword at his side.

Gaston moved silently, pouring ale into each of the cups set out on the table. The pitcher was large and awkward in his small hands, but he moved about the room as if he were a shadow. None of the men there paid him heed.

Impatient, I tried to look at each of their faces. Gaston was not of a mind to do that, though, and as I exerted a tendril of pressure, the pitcher tilted in his hand. Only quick movement on his part sent the wash of ale to the floor and not onto the Templar for whom he'd been pouring. I felt his confusion as he wondered what had happened.

"Have a care. If you wet my boots, you'll pay heftily." His meaty fist rose with menace. A tremor of fear went through the boy.

Aine spread my view of the room so that I could see the men I had been trying to get Gaston to look at. I didn't recognize any of the faces. All were intent on the food and drink laid out on the table. Eggs, fish, cheese, and sausage were arrayed with several loaves of bread and a jar of honey. Although the establishment was rough, these men were obviously treated with deference.

The strange drink in my body had an odd, calming effect. Normally, this type of read would open my mind to the emotions of all of the room's occupants, but it was not so this time. As I was marveling, the door to the hallway opened, and all eyes seemed to turn in that direction. When at last Gaston lifted his gaze to take in the newest arrival, I was struck a near physical blow. Without the benefit of time to recover, I was hit again.

"Get out."

THE FACE OF EVIL

Gaylen's exclamation was joined with a solid palm to the table. Gaston jumped at the quick violence, and I could feel his indecision. *No, stay.* I put everything into the push, but this was not the kind of link that worked that way. He moved toward the door, still reluctant, but moving. My heart dropped. I knew that I had lost him.

The knowledge infuriated and frightened me, and I released Aine's hands and made for the door, but Bertrand barred the way and Aine had a strong hold on my tunic. "Stop, Tormod. Ye risk yer brother's life if ye don't let this meeting follow its course," Bertrand said firmly.

I knew his words to be true, but it was a sore trial to heed him. The call of the Holy Vessel was strong. Though I could not feel Gaylen's presence, I felt the Vessel, and I knew he had it. To be this near and not wrest it from his body and make him pay for the nightmare of his previous trespass was torture.

Aine's song rose in my head and when I felt the need begin to grow less insistent, I slammed up my shields to her. I would not be whispered into forgetting he was here.

Aine recoiled as if I had struck her. Long moments pulsed between us. Then a soft knock at the door broke the tension. Bertrand put up a warning hand for silence, and Aine and I backed away from the sight of whoever waited there. He opened the door a sliver, then reached quickly into the hall and jerked the visitor in.

Gaston's gasp was sharp, and I exhaled abruptly.

"I have been dismissed by one of the party." His guilt for failing in his duties hung over him like a foul smell. "I found nothing. I thought ye should know that I'd been put out, so that ye could follow another path."

Gaston had found far from nothing. He had located the one person I detested more than any other in the whole of the world, the one I would gladly kill if I had the chance. "It's all right," I said. "There was nothing ye could have done."

"Have ye seen this one before, lad?" asked Bertrand.

"*Non*, this is the first time he has been here," he replied.

"We have to get into that room," I said, beginning to pace in the confined area. "We need to hear what's said."

"I will read the room once they have gone. Ye an' Bertrand will follow Gaylen when he leaves. I will catch up to ye when I can." Aine seemed to have it all worked out, except for the part that there was no way I was leaving this to her and slinking away.

"Alone? With a tavern full o' cutthroats below an' no idea where ye are?"

"Aye." Her answer held challenge. "I can find my way."

"Ye know it's a bad idea. We have to stay together." I was frustrated. "There has to be something we can do." Aine dropped heavily onto the pallet, and Bertrand went back to his chair, a resigned expression flattening the furrows above his brow.

"I'd best go below before I am missed," said Gaston. "I'll be back for your trenchers when I can. I'll tell them you need more ale." I handed him a copper to cover the expense, and he was out the door, a shadow in silence.

As the door swung shut behind him, I caught it, grabbed my cloak, and moved beyond it. "I'm going to have a look around," I mumbled. Aine's protest followed me into the empty hallway, where I drew the dark wool about me and ducked into the hood. The need to hold the carving was so heady I nearly hesitated before their door, but the soft murmur of voices and the thought of Torquil kept me moving past.

AN EAR TO THE WIND

The end of the hall was in near darkness, and the window I had seen from below easily swung open at my touch. The bite of cold air filled my chest as I leaned out and laid my hands on the overlapping boards. They were moist and rough beneath my fingers, and I clenched the wood tight.

Climbing out was not as simple as it seemed. My feet touched the edge of the boards just as a wind whipped across the side of the inn, and the shutter banged against its mooring. I moved quickly, crablike along the outer wall, hoping and praying that no one would come to investigate, while my uncooperative cloak billowed and tangled around my legs. In moments, I was cursing the quick impulse that had allowed me no time to think through this plan. The ground below was farther away than I had anticipated, and though I vowed to hold my eyes level and not look down, the oath proved difficult to keep.

Only thoughts of Torquil and the carving kept me moving. Pressing my boots hard to the wood, I badly missed the toes that I'd lost to the freezing sickness. The windows at the back of the inn were farther away than I'd thought.

As I climbed around the corner, voices drifted toward me from the nearest room. My calf was cramping, and I began to sweat. It was then that de Nogaret's voice rang in my ears. "I don't care what it takes, you bring me proof and I will see to the results." His words hung in the air, and darkness crept around the edges of my vision. "No," I whispered. "Don't let it take me. Lady, please."

I fought against the encroaching vision with a will I had never known. My fingers were white and grasping tight to the edge of the wood, sending splinters into my skin.

Men in the dark. The clink of sword and mail rustling. De Nogaret in the lead. *"Spread out and make sure no one escapes."*

My fingers were loosing. Fear beat at the edge of the blackness, pressing the vision away, and yet in its place a tremble of weakness shook my arms and legs. I looked at the ground so far away below me, and a swirl of dizziness whipped through me.

Tormod. Aine was suddenly in my head, her song giving me strength, her read of the situation immediate. I blinked in the darkness, my heart beating painfully, my fingers and legs burning.

It's useless. I canno' hold on. I felt faint and weak as the threat of a second vision pressed the back of my eyes. I fought it off with all of my strength.

Stay with me, Tormod. Help is on the way. A length of rope slithered down the side of the inn, and I felt rather than saw the small body that slipped over the edge of the roof. Gaston was like an animal of the forest: quick, steady, and fearless. He was beside me, looping the rope around my waist and tying it off nearly before I knew what he was doing. "Transfer your hands to the rope, monsieur. Bertrand will pull you up," he whispered.

My fingers were growing numb and my grip on the wooden slats was lessening. One hand slipped, and in my quick twist to right it, the rope around me cinched painfully tight.

"Here. Take hold," Gaston coached me softly, slipping the rope into my fingers and wrapping my hand tight. "Slowly. We go together."

STRENGTH IN NUMBERS

"That was the most asinine thing I ever witnessed. What were ye thinking?" Aine hissed, as I lay on a bale of hay in the animal byre a short while later. Gaston had gone back to his duties, and Aine and Bertrand sat beside me, the former attending the welts the rope had given my sides and hands. Through the cracks in the slanted wooden slats above my head, the light of the stars beckoned. With Aine's song still ringing in my ears, the worst of my recovery was over.

"Thank ye, Bertrand," I croaked. Aine's wide and furious stare pinned me to the straw. I owed her thanks, it was true, but I could not make myself say it aloud for the mood she was in.

"I had to know what was happening, Aine. We didn't have time to waste waiting for them to leave." My teeth were chattering. The cold air had worked its way around the chinks in the walls, and I had taken off my tunic to be examined by Bertrand.

"Was it worth it?" she muttered. "Ye're lucky Gaylen did no' know ye were there. I canno' imagine how ye got away with it." Aine was fuming and perhaps she had the right to, but I could hardly waste the time or energy on it right now. I stared hard at the wood above me as if it held the answers I sought.

"What is it, lad? What did ye see?" Bertrand asked.

"I saw de Nogaret leading soldiers through the night, to a place I've no' seen before." I shook my head and sighed. "But I feel as if I *should* know it."

"They are leaving." Gaston's head popped into the byre. "Some are off to the castle, others to the preceptory."

"Gaylen?" I asked.

He glanced toward Aine, hesitating. "He slipped away. While you were being pulled onto the roof."

The news was crushing. I'd already felt the distance between the carving and myself growing, but the knowledge that it was truly once again gone squeezed my heart. I stood and dressed quickly. "Let's go in," I said to Aine. "While it's all still fresh."

The room was cold and dark. As I waited for Gaston to light the half-burned candle, I noticed a draft. I crossed to the window as Aine's hum spread out over the room. The shutters were ajar, and I opened them wide and called on the power of the land to expand the vision, including Bertrand in our sight. The dimness instantly came to life with the pale ghostlike images of the bodies that had recently been there.

The Templars sat in chairs around the table. One stood by the window, his hand resting on the ledge as he gazed beyond the trees across the river. There were no lights over the land. Paris was shut up for the night, battened down against the damp mist that hung on the water.

"*Close the shutters, man. I'm near frozen,*" de Nogaret snapped. I turned and looked at the image of him, committing his features to my memory. What I saw did not impress me. Though he was, no doubt, rich and influential, I could read the cruelty and pettiness I had already witnessed through Gaston's memories.

The Templar by the window quickly turned from his post, absently drawing the shutters closed, not bothering to secure the latch. I released the breath I didn't realize I'd been holding. I had worried that they had heard or seen me outside.

I moved to the window and looked down. Sure enough, my ghosted image clung to the slats beneath the window across the way. I had been more than lucky.

My gaze returned to the room's interior, and as I focused toward the table I saw and heard Gaylen. "*Let us proceed.*" With his dagger he cut a hunk of the cheese from the wedge on the table.

De Nogaret appeared to bristle at Gaylen's taking charge, and led the conversation as if it had begun before Gaylen's arrival. "*You're certain you can trust the men chosen?*" he asked of the Templar seated quietly at the table. This knight was older than the rest, though not by much. Broad shouldered and strong, he wore the Templar mantle easily and intellect shone in his eyes. "*Of course,*" he replied.

"It is not an easy thing to gain the ear of the Pope. We will have but one chance, and all must be in place well before," de Nogaret said.

"Difficult, even if he is a friend of the King?" said the Templar near the window. He was the youngest. His face was barely whiskered, and his body had yet to fill out the shape of a knight. He was petulant and clearly not at ease.

De Nogaret's cold gaze pinned the man in place. "The King has no role in these proceedings. Is that clear?"

The man dropped his eyes. "Oui, milord."

Gaylen spoke then. "The evidence must be unquestionable. If 'tis brought to the highest o' courts, there must be little doubt in the minds o' those who will pronounce sentence. They have many friends who will seek to intercede on their behalf. It must be recorded an' undeniable."

"They are powerful," mumbled the youngest, chafing the beads at his waist, clearly afraid to speak again. "If any should find out our part in this, our lives will be forfeit."

"Your reward will be well worth the risk," said de Nogaret, dismissing the danger.

"And what of the other task you have been

assigned?" de Nogaret asked Gaylen. *"You have promised delivery of the artifact."*

Gaylen's hand dropped beneath the table, and he seemed to unconsciously touch the bundle tied at his waist. *"The Abbot has hidden it away. Tell the priest to question him about it. I have enough to arrange. I delivered the boy — my part in that is finished."*

I felt the heat of the carving flare at the mention of Torquil. Who had him? The Abbot? The unknown priest?

"Your part is fulfilled when we say it is. You require a favor of the King. It would be wise if you still have such a need to continue to seek the artifact. If it is in the hands of the Order, we cannot hope to succeed in this endeavor," said de Nogaret.

They stared at one another, a battle of wills to discern which was the more powerful. My wager would lie on Gaylen. I did not believe de Nogaret had any idea who he was dealing with.

The information we read here was important. Far more than any other vision I'd had so far.

"Establish contact with the Pope's man," said de Nogaret. *"And find out where that artifact lies."*

"Do no' presume to tell me where my duty lies," said Gaylen. *"Do yer part an' I will do mine."*

De Nogaret stood as if to challenge, and Gaylen raised his hand, a motion for silence. He cocked his head and his face became still, his eyes alert and darting. He glanced toward the beams above his head and stood, his hand going for the sack at his waist. *"I will contact ye when I know more."*

Aine dropped her link with the room's memories. I felt faint. The air seemed to grow colder, and I drew my cloak strongly about me. "He knew I was there," I said. "An' yet he did no' seek me out. Why?" I asked.

"He had the carving with him. He knows now a little o' what it can do. He is perhaps no' ready to do battle with ye again an' take the chance on losing it," said Bertrand. "I need to go to the preceptory an' tell the Grand Master what we've seen here. We know no' what it means, but none o' it is good."

"We should all go," I said.

"Nay, lad. We canno' take the chance that this is a trap. There is no way to know how many are on the side o' these." He snuffed the candle, and the room dropped into darkness.

THE HUNTER
OR THE HUNTED

We waited in the cold — damp, tired, and far away from any place safe enough to lay our heads. The docks on the water's edge smelled of dead fish and old leaves. Aine's cloak was pulled up and pressed tight to her face. "I'm sorry about before," she mumbled, her voice thick behind the wool.

I tilted my head, questioning.

"I shouldn't have gone into the room a' the inn alone. 'Twas only for a moment," she insisted. "But I *was* almost caught. One o' the Templars came up before the others."

I grimaced, but made a bid for peace. " 'Tis over. Ye're safe." I stared out over the lightly rippling water to the shore. "I am no one to speak badly o' taking chances," I said. "I *was* found out, an' it was all for naught. I didn't even learn anything from going out the window. It could have been far worse. It still might." Thoughts of Torquil in danger taunted me. Aine moved close and for a moment leaned against my side. The quiet comfort only she could give was welcome.

Gaylen knew that I had been on the roof and that the captive de Nogaret and the King assumed to be me was my brother. He could have given me up and earned extra favors from the King, but he hadn't. It was not out of goodwill; that was a surety. If Bertrand was right and Gaylen hadn't wanted to face me directly for fear of losing the carving, there was still the strong possibility that he was at this moment arranging for our arrest.

In the distance, I could see the dark shape of the ferryboat that would take us across the river. The night was quiet, and the regular soft dip of the oars marked its passage. The power of the land was a low ebb that shifted with the lap of water. I drew a strand to myself and reached to survey the boat. Only one man was aboard, and his thoughts were barely on us. We were his last fare. Drink and company awaited his return.

My neck was stiff with the persistent shiver that trembled along my back. Winter was growing closer by the day. I did not allow myself to linger on the thought of what would happen if we did not find Torquil soon. Aine pressed the back of her hand against mine, her silent support a blessing.

A few moments later, the boat beached with the soft stir of muddy silt. Aine boarded first, then Bertrand. I did a quick scan of the town behind us and the water ahead, then stepped carefully into the shell. My scan would not reach the opposite shore or any that might await us there, but for the moment I thought us to be safe. If Gaylen were watching or intent on following, though I would not be able to sense his presence, I would feel the carving. Since I didn't believe he would ever leave it behind and I felt no trace of it, I allowed myself a moment's peace.

The ferryman dug in his oars and pushed off. The wash of the river's current moved us along. It was black as pitch on the water, and the sound of the oars as they dipped was mesmerizing. Somewhere off to our left lay the Île de la Cité and the castle of the King, a threat that was now far closer and more real than ever before. Our hunters were near.

The Templars, Gaylen, and de Nogaret. It appeared to me that the only link between them was the Holy Vessel and myself, but there had to be more, something that lay right there before my eyes. De Nogaret demanded proof. Proof of what? That the Holy Vessel existed? No — the Templars, the Church, Gaylen, and the soldiers who were in the cave where I found the Holy Vessel's bowl, all knew that it was real. So that was not it.

Across the water, birds of the night fluttered and called. I let my body relax and my eyes haze. A voice came to me then, as unexpected as it was unknown.

"But I don't want to go to England and marry a man I have not met. He can't make me do it!"

"*There now, milady, if it happens you'll have no choice in the matter. You've known this all your life.*"

"*It's barbaric. Is this not the year 1307? Have we not come further than this? When I marry, it will be for l'amour.*"

A chuckle sounded in my mind. "*You will be lucky if the man your father chooses is kind and wise. Love is for the peasants, milady.*"

"*If I were a peasant, then freedom would be mine.*" The flash of a bright amber gaze filled the dark of my mind's eye, and as it faded I found myself staring into a different set of eyes. Eyes that held a spark of annoyance.

Aine said nothing, just turned away and closed her eyes. Suddenly, her shielding was stronger than moments before, and she was closed off to me.

I tucked my arms around myself and wondered what in the world had brought on this vision? The lass was lovely. I found myself lingering over the color of her eyes and the shape of her face. Though the conversation was forgettable, the lass was not.

Aine's eyes opened, and I felt her stare. I shook my head and turned my thoughts to the carving, the base of the Vessel. The mysterious wooden talisman had been fashioned by one of the gifted in the likeness of his mother. He had been a Protector, but I knew no more of their tale, save that the woman was somehow linked to the carving, and that her spirit came to me in times of need and enhanced the gifts I was born with.

I called her face to mind and silently asked what it was she wanted of me? What were these riddles I was meant to find the answer to? A glow of warmth came to me then, pressing away the chill. It was not an answer, but it gave me hope.

Aine was seated close by, huddled against the cold. I drew some of the heat that I had been granted and whispered it in her direction. Her eyes drowsily held mine, and she nodded a silent thanks as we drifted across the river.

A PARTING OF WAYS

No one waited on the opposite shore. Though I knew it long before we beached, I was still surprised that Gaylen hadn't arranged an armed welcome. Aine's hum filled the back of my mind, and I automatically reached for the one who had rowed us here. *No passengers traveled this crossing.* I drew on a strand of power that glistened on the air and gently set to blurring the edges of his memories.

We moved away into the darkness of the trees, and I opened my mind to the area around us. Beech and elm grew thickly, and as I walked, the ancient feel of the forest swirled about my senses. It was different here. I understood now what Aine had detected; there was a sluggishness to the beat of life.

Aine was wrapped tight in her woolen cloak. Misery, cold, and exhaustion had grown within her since leaving the boat, and I noticed that she stumbled over the gnarled roots at our feet more than she would have normally. The night sky was a somber gray, as if the promise of the coming day's light was not assured.

"We part ways here," said Bertrand. "I'll be in touch as soon as I know something. Be careful ye both." An odd chill skittered along my spine, and my skin tingled.

I nodded, and Aine and I turned away, following a path that was no more than a small break in the foliage as Bertrand continued west.

Aine had reached the top of the hill, and she looked down toward the direction Bertrand had disappeared. I could see the vague outline of the Templar preceptory off in the distance. Aine murmured something softly.

"Aye?" I prompted.

"Ye didn't do what ye usually do. That 'stay true to the light' bit ye Templars always say whenever ye part ways," she said before she turned away and started down the backside of the hill.

It was in me suddenly to run after Bertrand, to send him off with the Templar blessing. I felt badly for not thinking to do it. I was not a Templar as yet, but had witnessed Alexander share the well wish and had adopted it since we'd parted. I hadn't been at all diligent about my devotions on this journey. My prayers were done in moments of haste and need. I was a poor apprentice, I thought, and silently said the words toward the direction he had gone.

I started down the hill then, eager for the solace that sleep would bring. Aine and I were alone. Again. The sudden realization struck me, and I looked at her sidelong. She was just a black shape in the darkness. Without a word, she slowed and moved closer, tangling her fingers with my own. The breath I hadn't realized I'd been holding released on a sigh.

She shivered, and the ripple of it passed through her hand where it met mine. "Are ye cold?" I made to undo my cloak.

"No. 'Tis this land. I don't know what is wrong with it, but the power is strange. Twisted and weaving in a way that I have never come across before," she murmured. "Though, granted I've no' been far." I hadn't noticed that she was scanning the area around us. Her mind's touch was subtle. "Ye've been to this place before, aye?" she asked.

"No' here specifically, but in this land, aye," I said, opening my senses more widely to try and understand what she was sensing.

"There are so many echoes o' the lives that have passed here. Their stories jump into my head," she said. "But 'tis more than that — I've known that feeling the whole o' my life. Here there is a twisted kind o' squambly feeling that grips my inners whenever I let the echo roll over me. 'Tis like the power is off. Wrong somehow an' 'tis warping my read." It was more words from her than I had heard in several days.

"Is it a worry, d'ye think?"

"I don't know. Maybe 'tis just a different kind o' power here than a' home," she said.

Home. The word gave me a sudden jolt of longing for the way it used to be, under the roof of my parents, surrounded by my brothers and sisters and not haring off across a strange land on a quest that I still had no great understanding of.

"It makes me want to fix it somehow," Aine said, drawing me back. She hummed softly as we walked, and I listened with all of my senses, normal and gifted. "But I don't know how to do it, an' I'm fair frightened to try," she said.

The power all around us *was* different from home. The air was cool, and yet the strands that drifted along its edges were thick and somehow sticky and hot. I could not direct them to shift as I could at home. They clung to my mind's touch, leaving something behind when I dropped the link.

"I sense what ye mean, but I don't have any thought as to how we could change it or even if we should," I said. Even with the strengthened bond between the Holy Vessel and myself, this seemed beyond me.

Aine said nothing, just wandered the road with her head cocked and her song playing softly in the night.

ON OUR OWN

The inn that we found was in a small village whose name I did not mark. The dwelling was one of many such dark, wooden hovels scattered among the hills. Though it stood on its own, it projected the air that if one board should crack, the whole would tumble down in a heap of tinder. A small, wooden plaque hung from a rusted-iron spike over the door. It's marking was nearly as dark as the weathered plank it was made from, but I could vaguely make out a crudely carved crown. This was the place Bertrand had suggested.

It was dim and quiet, shut up for the night. Aine stood behind me, tightly tucked up in her cloak. The drift of her hum played softly in my mind. I rapped on the door.

A woman opened it several long moments later. She was as thin as a stripling. Her gray hair hung in strands down her face and was caught up in the back with some sort of rough twine. "What do you want?" Her voice was as haggard as the rest of her.

"We need a room," I said. Beneath the words I wove a suggestion. *Open the door an' show us in. Ask no questions. Remember only a tinker man.*

Without a word she turned, leaving the door ajar. Aine and I slipped inside. The main room was sparse, and smelled of fires long banked with ale. *A meal,* I whispered.

She handed us two wooden bowls and silently ladled a thick, pasty soup into them from an iron pot that hung over a low fire, then she fetched us wine in heavy, clay mugs. I whispered to her once more, and we were shown to a room off the main before she disappeared back to her own with no memory of having served or seen us.

Aine dropped to the pallet and slowly began to eat, her exhaustion so strong that her arm fell to her lap after each bite, as if it weighed two stone.

I took a small, heavy stool by the door. The soup had been long cooking. The taste of the burned bottom of the pot ran through the thickness so strongly, I could not recognize what had been used for meat or vegetable. I ate it nonetheless. We had traveled hard and eaten little.

Aine finished and was swaying where she sat. "Sleep," I said. "I will take the watch."

"Do we need a watch?" she murmured, dropping flat and drawing the coverlet close. "No' a soul knows that we are here."

I didn't bother to answer. Gaylen knew that we were somewhere in this land, and I would not be taken by him unaware. Aine's even breathing told me she had slipped off.

I moved the stool against the wall, and in the clear space I drew my dagger from its sheath. I was amazed, as always, at the feel of it in my hand and the knowledge that it was precious and mine. It had been the Templar's, an Islamic work of art he had gifted me with. Quietly, I murmured the prayer of Our Lady and deftly moved through the exercises the Templar had taught me. The rhythm of the prayer helped me keep time, but it did nothing to settle my unease. I could not dispel the feeling that Gaylen was about to make my life even more difficult than it had been of late.

Exercises done, I pulled a scrap of worn linen from my bag and wiped the sweat from my neck and face. Though Aine would most likely not appreciate it if she woke, I approached the room's small window, pushed aside the shutter, and stuck my head out into the night. Beyond the walls, the air was filled with wetness. I leaned into it, grateful for the cool that pushed aside my fatigue.

The wind had risen. The cold held the sharp scent of snow and winter. A storm was coming, a maelstrom not unlike the one already raging within me, and it had everything to do with Gaylen, de Nogaret, and the Templars. I was beyond my abilities. I needed the help of Templar Alexander in this. Although I knew it was dangerous to use the power in a way that would ripple the web, I called to him.

Alexander. Please. If ye can hear me, speak. I put all of my desperation into the call, drawing the power and fueling the reach. The currents stirred beneath my feet, as if waking from a long slumber, and tingled along my shielding. The wind blew cold through my hair and pressed against my neck like a blade freshly sharpened. The Templar was out there somewhere, if only I could find him. I drew to mind all that was his essence, his peace, his strength. It was more than I had ever attempted before, and I felt as if my mind were spreading thin.

And then as if he had never been away, I felt the link that we had once shared flare to life. Joy burst within me. I had thought it forever broken.

Where are ye? I asked.

Close, came the reply. *Stay. Wait.* Mindspeech was less trackable, when you used the least amount of words fueled by small bursts of power. I had forgotten.

Torquil? I asked. Instantly, a series of images flit before my mind's eye. Black walls. Manacles. Rusted chain. In a panic I tried to move closer, to follow the path of his thoughts, but I was cut off abruptly.

Safe. The Templar's reassurance was strong, and his peace flowed through me. *Only a possible future.*

What d'ye mean? I nearly shouted, breaking the rule, lengthening my words. But my thought seemed to echo uselessly in my mind. Our contact had begun to fade. In moments, it dropped away altogether.

My body swayed, and I clutched the wall. The thought of my brother in chains made me feel ill . . . but what had I expected? I must take heart. Torquil was alive and the Templar was coming.

I secured the shutter, finding it difficult to raise my arm to do it. The contact was taking its toll, but I didn't care in the least.

I crossed to the pallet and looked down on Aine. I wanted to wake her and tell her what happened, but she slept so peacefully that I found I could not. Her red ringlets were short and bright on the coverlet. Without thinking, I reached down and rubbed a lock between my fingers. It was as soft as I remembered. Aine shifted and the bit of hair slipped away.

I moved the stool close to the bed and sat down. It was not a surprise when her eyes opened and she slid back, making room, and beckoned with an outstretched hand.

So tired. I moved as if in a dream, taking my place beside her. Her eyes were luminous in the candlelight. Gently, her arm lifted and I felt the trace of her fingers on my face. I closed my eyes to rest, yet it was as if a trail of fire sparked along my jaw. With it, a wash of memory slid through me. Moments we had spent alone, just like this. Aine was remembering and I, in my exhaustion, was reading her. I felt her breath fan softly across my lips, and all but the need to kiss her emptied from my mind. Gently, I pressed my lips to hers. I had forgotten how soft they were, how incredible the sensation of her closeness was.

Aine reached out and cupped my face, holding me still while her mouth explored the edges of my own. There was no fear in her now, no nervousness. She rolled to her back, and I moved with her, our bodies pressed close. It felt good, right, as if we were two halves to a whole.

"Tormod?" Hesitation colored her tone.

"Aye?" I said.

"Have ye seen that vision before?"

It took a moment for me to understand which vision she was talking about. It was the girl I had seen when we crossed the river. Something large seemed to weigh on the answer I would give.

"No. 'Twas fair odd, eh? No' something I should think would be part o' anything coming to me."

"Aye," she said softly, fumbling with the coverlet. "Comely, she was, don't ye think?"

I was so tired I barely attended her words. "Aye. Beautiful," I replied absently.

"I wouldn't say that exactly," she said, "but no' plain."

"Aye."

Her arms circled my back, and I buried my face in her neck, feeling the pulse of her blood roar beneath my face. *I love ye, Tormod.* Aine's words brushed my mind. And everything within me stilled. She hadn't meant for me to hear. I was linked to her. Suddenly, I thought of the Templars and the life I had always wanted to lead, a life that did not include women, a life without Aine.

I felt the shock run through her, the hurt and disbelief. Immediately, I drew up the shielding around me,

73

severing my thoughts from hers, but the damage had already been done. She had pulled away from me, backed as far away on the pallet as she could manage, like a frightened animal.

I wanted to draw her back into my arms, to explain that Templar life had been all I had ever thought of, it had always been my only desire. I didn't know what I wanted anymore.

I drew myself from the pallet and turned away into the cold of the room. Her shields were still low, and I could feel her hurt and confusion. "Close yer eyes," I whispered. "Get some sleep."

I heard the rustle as she turned onto her side, and in moments I was no longer privy to her thoughts or feelings. Aine had shut me out. A ripple of pain squeezed my heart. I forced myself to move away — to take the stool once more. I drew my dagger and held it loosely, facing the door. What good I might have been if Gaylen or some other threat had burst through, we were lucky enough not to know.

MIXED MESSAGES

Aine woke early and didn't speak a word to me as she washed her face and hands in a basin by the door. I moved to the pallet in her place and closed my eyes. The coverlet was warm with the heat of her body and smelled faintly of her hair. My insides were twisted with the oddness that now lay between us. I heard her moving about the room but did not dare lift an eyelid to see what she was about.

The door opened and closed. I cast a glance toward it. Though I worried briefly about where she had gone and what trouble she might get into, I closed my eyes and welcomed sleep.

Men in shadow, clustered together. Flickering candlelight. *"His name is Beaton. Wasn't that the name linked to Alexander Sinclair and the boy?"*

I jerked awake with a bolt of panic. The voice was that of the Templar trainee, the older of the three working with de Nogaret and Gaylen.

Bertrand was discovered or would be soon. I rose quickly and threw our packs together, hoisted both across my back, and headed down the hall to the common room. It was empty, and a flicker of annoyance rolled through me.

Aine knew how dangerous it was to be out alone, and yet she had taken off nonetheless. Around the inn, I felt the sleep-dampened thoughts of the occupants as they began to rouse for the day.

She was not out back, where only a trough of water and some bundles of hay marked the stable area. Nor was she in the storage shed or in the main room. I was beginning to worry. Thinning my shields, I felt for her presence along the net of power that glistened in the early light. When I felt nothing, a tight knot grew inside me. If something were wrong, I would sense it, I told myself. If she were near, I would sense her. So why then did absence of both fill me with such unease? I lingered in the shadow of the inn's drooping roof. This was not the time for her to go haring off. We needed to probe the dream and find out what more we could.

Time seemed to drag as I waited and my worry for Bertrand grew. It was hard to believe that Aine would leave me without a word, but where was she? My breath floated cold on the air before me and I shivered.

Her childish game was frustrating. She was angry with me and went off somewhere to brood, severing our link to each other, so that I could not probe her through the power.

I made one last round of the inn, ending back in the room. "Fine. Have it yer way," I mumbled. "I didn't ask ye to come along in the first place." I couldn't leave a note — she could not read — so she'd just have to make what she would of it and wait. I thumped her bag on the pallet.

It was only after I had walked for over a candle mark that I remembered the Templar's command that I stay and wait for his arrival. Aine would be there, I told myself. He would find her, and I would be back with Bertrand before anything went amiss.

DESPERATE MEASURES

The stone wall of the preceptory was strong and fortified by a great many turrets spaced regularly by the walkways between. There was only one enormous wooden gate, and two knights stood guard on the parapet above it. From my vantage at the edge of the forest, I watched the latest rotation of the change in guard. The knights arriving were no less alert or fearsome than the ones they replaced, and I felt my resolve waver.

It was one thing to enter a preceptory under the protection of the Templar Alexander and entirely another to go in alone. I had no idea whether I would be welcomed or imprisoned and yet, for Bertrand I knew I must make the attempt.

Several carts came and went as I stood sentinel, thinking. I could not enter as myself and alert the ones who sought me. I could not just walk up to the gates and request a room.

A small weaver's cart approached from a distance, rolling along the rutted road. I watched it with half a mind. Its wheels were thin and spindly, lacking the iron rims of the heavier wagons. I doubted they would last long jouncing over the uneven terrain. I needed a way in. One that would take me past the eyes of the watchers.

The wheels were made of wood. Live trees. The Templar had taught me to look for life that remained within objects that had once been part of the weave of power. Although this wood had died and hardened long ago, if I could find just a memory of the life that had once resided there, I could work with it. I had once frayed rope in this way.

But I had to go carefully. To use power this close to the preceptory would be dangerous. The cart was nearing. If I was going to try, it would have to be now.

Quickly, I reached for the droplets of energy that hung softly on the edges of the trees. My heart sped, and a breeze riffled the tiny hairs up and down my arms. In my mind I pictured the front wheel of the cart, not as a solid thing, but the way it once was — a living, growing, bending stalk. Inside was the information of its past, the way it had been long ago, before man's hands had shaped and molded it. And it was there that I saw what I needed — the wheel's outer rim had a small knot of energy in the grain of the wood.

I drew moisture from the air and worked it through the tough outer layer and into the knot, forcing it into the small spaces that naturally occurred there. The splinter was faint, but with each turn of the wheel it grew. A loud crack, and the shout of the wagon's driver when the whole of it gave way in the next rut heralded my effort. In the confusion, I bolted from the trees and appeared at the driver's side, whispering the suggestion I had been planning.

An inconvenience. Good thing there were two of us. We will need to unload the wagon and carry the goods inside.

The driver had no thought for my sudden appearance, ordering me to deliver two of the bolts of linen to the Templar weavers and fetch the wheelwright while he saw to the horses. I was only too glad to comply — to the first of his requests, at least.

When I passed beyond the gate, I held the bolts high to hide my face and the moment I rounded the bend in the path beyond the granary, I laid them down in the late grass of the meadow and took off toward the main house as if I belonged.

There were many outlying buildings. I skirted several farms, stables, and worker houses along the way, keeping my head low and my eyes to the road. Bertrand had described the grounds to me. He would be staying at the dormitories, housed in a large building that encircled a central courtyard toward the northern edges. There were many workers in the preceptory, but I had to assume that not every one knew every other. I strode as if with great purpose. It would have been nice to use the power to cloak myself, but inside the preceptory the chance that I would be discovered far outweighed the risk.

There were fewer guards inside the grounds, and I found it easier to navigate than I had anticipated. Passing through an archway to the courtyard's interior, I encountered several knights in training. I dipped my head and they moved past, but not before I heard one speak.

"We will meet in the chapel, after weapons."

I glanced up from beneath my cowl. The voice was familiar, one I had heard only this morning. It was Zachariah, who had met with de Nogaret and the others in the room at the Cochon Rouge. His companions had been there as well. Two of the men nodded and turned aside, disappearing along an inner corridor. Zachariah continued across the grass, and I ducked into the shade of one of the many pillars that ringed the courtyard. After a moment, I followed.

The man was much into his own thoughts, for although I stayed close he never once looked behind. He passed through a second archway, and I followed. But when his soft footsteps moved to a set of stairs at the end of a long corridor and beyond my sight, I was forced to hang back a bit. This was no open hallway filled with bodies to blend in with. I was alone. Still, I silently crept in his wake. The stairs led to a maze of hallways and abandoned rooms, where doors were ajar and furniture had been stripped. A fine layer of dust lined the floor.

No one had passed this way but Zachariah in quite some time. I was easily able to track my way to the doorway he'd gone through.

Quickly, I slipped into the adjoining room, pressed my ear against the wall, and tried to make sense of the murmur of voices that came from the other side of it.

"What have ye to tell me that was so urgent it could not wait until we were assured of secrecy?" I was surprised. The other occupant must have entered from another direction.

"The healer who traveled with Sinclair arrived last night. He is seeking an audience with the Grand Master and asking questions about the Abbot from Scotland."

There was a weighted pause, and I held my breath. "Did he arrive alone?"

"There was no other," the trainee replied.

I heard the rustle of restless movement. "It could be a coincidence, but this is no' the time for chances. Far too much is a' stake."

"That is what I assumed you would say. The matter is already being taken care of."

I heard the clink of coin exchanged. "Ye will go far in this, lad. Yer service is noted."

My throat tightened. *Bertrand.* I slipped from my place and made my way quickly down the stairs. In the space of a moment, the preceptory had changed. This place of refuge no longer held the safety I had come to rely on. My hopes and dreams were somehow muddied in a wash of uncertainty. Templar Knights, plotting against one of their own. My friend.

Anger curled within me, and as I passed through the dark and dusty hallways, the power deep below the land seemed to pulse with my every footfall. Without reaching, I felt the essence that was Bertrand. The location echoed impressions that had somehow become stored within my memory, the smell of a cook fire and baking bread. I turned toward the scent. He was near the kitchens.

That I could sense him there was a comfort. My focus was absolute: Get Bertrand and get out. The road I followed was all but deserted. Swiftly, I passed the granary and the weavers, across a field and along the path between the workers' huts, careful to avoid being seen.

Several wagons were being unloaded near the kitchens. Workers were hurrying and hauling. As I passed the side of a cart, I lifted a full sack of turnips. "Be at it, quickly!" a man emerging from the kitchens urged. "There will be little time as it is to prepare the feast," he said. "His Eminence enjoys a meal that is overflowing."

I ducked beyond the wooden lintel and into the kitchen, which was a flurry of activity. Workers were peeling and chopping vegetables, plucking an assortment of fowl, and stoking the fire in a hearth that stretched the width of one entire wall. The smell of baking filled every corner of the room. I dropped the heavy sack beside others of its kind and before anyone could direct me toward another duty, I ducked through a doorway into a small corridor that smelled sharply of drying herbs. As I worked my way through the building, the feel of Bertrand grew stronger. Yet I had to move with caution — there were others near. Voices and the edge of panic wafted toward me on the currents of power stirring in my wake.

"I don't understand, he was well just a moment ago." The voice was one of the trainees who had been with Zachariah. "Put something beneath his head. Call a healer."

I began to move more quickly, the gift in me responding to someone in need.

"But he is a healer," murmured the first.

"Well, he's obviously not able to tend to himself. Call another." As I reached the door, a boy brushed past in a sprint. Behind him several men clustered around a body on the floor. "His breath has stopped." I slipped into the room, the power of the land seeping through the soles of my feet and washing through my body, readying for use.

The room was in half-light. Through the cluster of

people, the pale slackness of Bertrand's face leapt at me, and my heart seemed to stop. With little care to the consequences, I pushed through the gathered, dropped to his side, and grasped his hand. Beneath my fingers his skin was hot and moist and the power within me surged like the crash of a wave.

"Breathe!" The trainee was leaning over him, feeling along his neck and chest for signs of life. I felt the man drawing from the web haphazardly, but knew that his abilities were weak. He seemed to have no idea what to do. No one would sense my use of the power in the muddle he was making.

Quickly, I moved into the haze of other sight, opening my mind to the inner workings of Bertrand's body. His breath and the beat of his heart were slow.

Help me. I sent the call deep into Bertrand's mind as I examined the hot traces of red that lined his throat and reached deep into his stomach. I'd never seen anything like it before. The angry red was not just in those places, but had spread throughout the length and breadth of him. Bright splotches marred his inners and flowed in the blood pumping from his heart. Ill humors were circulating to every corner of his being.

Though the power was rolling through me, seeking out the wrongness, I felt resistance. The more I sought out the spots of red, the slower Bertrand's heart seemed to beat. I focused there, mentally squeezing the organ, expelling the blood, and encouraging it to beat faster, but it wasn't working. The moment I released it from my mental grasp, the heart went back to its labored pulsing. I could not make up the difference he needed. Bertrand's body was shutting down, going cold and still, one part at a time, and I could not stop it. Helplessness beat at my mind. How could this be happening?

The apprentice was frantic. "No! You must not die! Do you hear me?" His demands were loud. I felt like howling with him as well.

Tormod? The probe was soft, within my mind.

Aye, Bertrand, I'm here, I answered. *Tell me what to do, how to stop this!* His fingers were going cold in mine.

I am afraid. Pray with me.

Pray! No! Tell me what to do. I need help healing ye. My eyes swam.

It's too late. There is no healing that will make a difference, lad.

The shock of his words made my guts heave. Too late! It could not be. *But I can do it. I can heal ye. The power is here at my call.*

Need ye. Please. His voice was weak.

What can I do? Anything. Just show me an' I will do what is needed. I was desperate to help.

Want to go home, Tormod. Take me there.

Aye. Let's get out of here. Help me heal ye an' we can go home. I begged him.

No. My body is done. Take me there.

Understanding came to me all at once. There was nothing more I could do to heal him, but I could bring him comfort. *Our Father, who art in Heaven, hallowed be thy name,* I began, and within moments the beauty of the prayer whispered between us. I called upon images then of our land, Scotia: the roar of the sea, the golden pink of dawn creeping over the cliffs, mist lying deep over the dark purple lochs. I let them fill my mind and his as well.

As the prayer came to an end, Bertrand's eyes opened and fixed on mine. I felt his body go lax then, and as the life drifted out of him we shared one last memory: A man's pale blue eyes, faintly lined with age and knowledge. Bertrand was gone before I could ask why the Archbishop was the last man he thought of before he passed. Then everything within me wept.

"I'm sorry." The whisper of words barely brushed the air, but I heard them. The trainee's eyes were not on me when they were uttered, but they rose to mine as if he felt my pain across the body of my friend. My guts twisted with the sudden fury that overtook me.

"Here now. What's the commotion? Step back." An old man's voice heralded the arrival of a Templar healer, come too late to do any good. At his side were several knights and a bevy of the curious.

Immediately, I slammed my shields in place and edged my way back from the body. The trainee's eyes remained on me, his questions plain. Who was I? How much did I know? Guilt and fear rolled off him as I circled the onlookers. Then, just as I slipped through the door, I darted a look back at him and shoved a whisper hard into his unprotected mind. *Ye will pay for this.*

THE HEART'S LOSS

I could do nothing for Bertrand and although I wanted to stay and bury him with honor and dignity, there were things at stake now that demanded I keep my wits about me. The preceptory was no longer a place of safety. I had to get back to tell Aine what had happened. The ache in my chest grew wider when I thought about trying to speak the words to her. Bertrand was one of us. And now he was gone, and I had no reason why that should be so.

The animals of the forest stirred as I walked past, and the power of the land rippled beneath my feet. I drew a cloak of the glistening strands around me, cocooned in the warmth, comforted. My use of the power should have left me drained, but oddly enough I felt strong, renewed. Bertrand was gone. Another friend, another life taken. I didn't know him as well as I did the Templar, but his loss was keenly felt.

I was glad the road was empty, for I had not the heart for another confrontation, and my mind was much too occupied. The Templar trainees were up to something. They had killed Bertrand, I was certain of it, but I had little reason to believe it and less to prove it.

The inn was nearly deserted when I arrived. The woman who had given us our room stooped by the hearth, stacking new wood as an old man watched from a nearby bench. Neither spoke when I stepped inside, but a ripple in the web of power brought my steps to a halt.

My thoughts leapt to Aine. I reached for her quickly, sending my thoughts along a tendril of power, but there was no response. I hurried across the common room and into the one we had let. It was dark, and I moved to the shutter to let in some light.

"Did I no' tell ye to wait?"

I whipped about, my dagger in my hand and outstretched before I had even managed the thought. The words came from the shadow of a man seated in the corner. His cloak was drawn close, and his frame was smaller than my memory had painted it, but joy still rose in me. "Alexander?"

"Aye, lad." He stood as I crossed the room.

I couldn't believe that after all this time he was finally here. I didn't know what to do or say. We'd been through so much, and I'd missed him badly. Once I would have thrown my arms around his waist and hugged him as I would have my da, but so much had happened. I was no longer that person, that bairn that I was at the very beginning of all of this.

He made it easy. He clapped my back strongly and grasped my forearms as one Brother of the Order would have another. I returned the embrace. "It's good, a' last, to see ye, my friend," he said.

"Better to see ye, Alexander," I replied. The feel of welcome and safety he projected made me breathe more comfortably. His gaze passed over me, as mine did him. I was surprised at what I found. I could scarce believe that his hair had as much silvery gray as it did. It had not been so long a time. I was shocked by his appearance. He seemed far older. His cheeks were sunken, and he was thin.

"How are ye?" I asked, deeply concerned.

"I am as well as I could be, an' far better than I might. I would no' be here a' all if it were no' for you."

His words reminded me. "Bertrand . . ." I began, and was embarrassed to feel my eyes begin to tear.

He nodded, his face filled with sadness. "I foresaw what happened, but I had hoped an' prayed that it would be otherwise."

"I arrived too late to discover what truly was going on or to do anything to stop it." Guilt was thick within me.

"Ye did what ye could, lad. Bertrand went home in peace to the Lord." He drew away and sat heavily on the stool by the table.

"But I was no' able to save him, to use my healing abilities." I could barely meet his eyes.

"Tormod. The Lord asks many things o' us, but nothing we are unable to give. What ye gave Bertrand was more than any other would have been able. Every man does what he must. Ye do well with the gifts ye've been given."

Just speaking to him made me feel better. "Ye came to me in my time o' need, called upon the Lord, an' were granted a miracle," he said. "Yer heart full o' goodness brought me back when I thought that I never would see another sunlight."

"But I used the power for myself to heal ye. I let all o' those men see it an' now 'tis known. I have failed. All the other carriers have kept it secret. I have let the knowledge o' the Holy Vessel's existence out into the world, where 'tis now in jeopardy. I saw a gathering o' the Order in a vision talking about it. They were angry with me."

"Everything we do has its price," he said.

Something in his words brought my thoughts back to Aine. Her pack was gone. "Was Aine here when ye arrived?" I asked.

"She was no'," he replied.

Though there was no censure in his tone, I bristled nonetheless. "Well, I could no' just sit here an' wait until she decided to come back from wherever she'd gone off to." I looked away, uncomfortable having to defend myself to him this way.

"Ye made a choice, Tormod. I do no' fault ye in that. I told ye once that all we do has consequences attached. This is one. We must make our future decisions based upon it."

A tankard of ale sat untouched on the table. "If ye would, fetch us something to eat. We have many things to discuss an' a tale to catch up on."

I nodded and made for the door, though the questions were teeming within me. "D'ye think she's all right?" I asked. A cold lump filled my stomach. Already I missed the peace that came with her presence and touch.

"I have seen where she may eventually turn up." He

made a grimace, apparently displeased with the information. "But what might befall her before then I canno' say."

For once his words did not make me feel better. "Food, Tormod?" he asked.

"Aye," I mumbled.

I returned to the common room deep in thought. Aine was gone. Bertrand was as well. It was only the Templar and myself, as it was in the beginning, together again. But this time things were not the same.

PART TWO

A REUNION LONG OVERDUE

"Tell me o' Torquil," I asked. I'd fetched a meal of hot stew for the both of us, and we tucked into the pitcher of ale after the Templar had spoken the prayer of thanks. Now I could wait no more.

"He is alive an' that is something for which we must be thankful. I tracked them as far as the Scotia Coast, where they put him aboard a merchant ship bound for this coast. I was unable to board but followed in a Templar ship that left on the following tide." His gaze on me was steady. "They arrived before me, but my sources cannot confirm where he was taken then."

It was as if he had thrust a dagger into my guts. All that I had eaten surged to my throat. I saw Torquil again in the dark, pain stripping his mind bare. He cried out, so tortured that it was agony to hear. I grabbed my ears to keep it away.

The Templar was beside me then, his hands on my head. "Push it away, Tormod. Filter it out an' shift it into the earth."

I had forgotten the most basic of my lessons, but at his urging performed the triple shielding with half a heart. Why should I be spared witnessing what my brother would endure in my name? Still it was a relief when the vision slid away.

"They will kill him," I murmured. "Lash him until the pain destroys him. All without knowing that he is no' me." I moved toward the door, more than ready to trade my life in exchange for his.

"No, lad. That will help no one," he said. "We will go there an' do all we can to prevent this from happening. Though I know no' the specifics, I have a sense of the timing. All o' the indicators I have seen tell me that this has no' an' will no' happen for a while."

I made to shrug him off, but he held my arms in an unyielding grip. "This is one o' the things that might never come to be, if we are able to ripple the waters of the future. We need to do this right, no' rush in unprepared."

All that had happened. All I'd seen and felt seemed a weight on my soul that drew me down onto the pallet's edge. "I will no' let him die in my place," I said flatly.

"We will do all that we can to keep that from happening," he said. "Come, gather yer things. There are preparations to be made."

When night fell, we left the inn. It was better to be cloaked in darkness than to venture out in daylight with a price on our heads. Together we made a larger target and yet we would not travel apart again. Our destination was a small house in the thick of Paris proper, found by way of a sequence of thin roads between tightly built dwellings.

"Where have ye been all o' this time?" I asked as we walked. "What happened after the caves?"

He was quiet a moment, seeming deep within himself. "I never expected that ye would return to the cave's entrance, once ye'd found what I had sent ye for. Ye took me much by surprise," he said.

"Ye weren't happy that I did," I replied, remembering the scene as if it had happened yesterday. I had found the beautiful wooden bowl and reunited it with the ancient carving that I had carried in his place. In return, I had been granted a series of visions — one that revealed that the Templar would fall beneath a blade in the very place I had left him. Desperate to keep that from happening, I had rushed to his side and leapt into the fray, only to cause the injury I had seen.

"Tormod, ye saved my life that day. Though I didn't want ye to return an' bring the Holy Vessel to a place where it might be taken from ye, if ye hadn't come I would have died."

"Aye, but had I no' returned, ye would no' have been caught unaware. 'Tis a wicked circle that I have struggled with for long an' away."

"I am here, an' 'tis thanks to ye." His eyes bored into mine. "I owe ye my life."

"I didn't know it had worked," I said. "I would never have left ye there, otherwise."

"Then let us be thankful that ye did no' know, for the Holy Vessel would surely be in the hands o' the King by now."

"'Tis no' in much better hands with Gaylen," I said.

"Don't blame yerself overmuch for that, Tormod. The carving called ye back to Her side. There is more that She intends for ye to do in Her service, an' She has, I think, plans o' Her own."

He lapsed into silence as we walked. The road had more travelers than before. We'd moved into a more thickly settled part of the town. "Ye think that all o' this is happening because o' the carving?" I asked. "That this ancient vessel is somehow moving all o' us around an' setting whatever it needs to have done in order?" It was a difficult thought, but one I had been trying to come to grips with. What was this thing and what was it asking of me? Was it for good or bad? Many had already died because it had thrust itself back into the hands of men.

"I think that something very large is beneath Her call. 'Tis up to us to discover what that is."

I drew my sack a little higher on my shoulder, jostled as we passed two men on the narrow road. "Where did ye go after the caves? Why did ye no' contact me?" I asked when once again we walked alone. The sting of hurt I could not conceal colored my words.

"Ahram an' his men took me to their lands. The great healer o' the sultan attended my wounds, but the cut was deep an' I'd lost a great deal o' blood. 'Twas no' an easy recovery." Pain shadowed his eyes. "I searched for ye, Tormod, the moment I could, but I was always just a bit too far behind. Our link changed when ye used the power. I could sense ye, but I could only contact ye when ye were in great danger an' yer mind was unfocused."

I remembered then the odd times I had heard his voice in my mind. I had thought it was my imagination. The Templar had been near all along, helping me through the worst of my trials. I shook my head in wonder.

" 'Twas good that I was behind, instead o' alongside ye, in the end, for I would no' have been near enough to track the soldiers when they took Torquil."

My thoughts were whirling. "Did ye know that Torquil was gifted?" I asked.

"Not a' the time, but I felt the ripple o' power when he whispered the men into believing that he was ye."

"I think he learned that from me on the boat. I had wondered why his questions were so pointed. But to have been able to do it without yer training is astounding." I wondered if the Templar had wished it had been Torquil who had been at the hut on that night long ago instead of me.

"Things go as they are meant to, Tormod."

I smiled to myself. He had always seemed to have the ability to pluck the very thoughts from my mind, though he'd never use that ability unless it was absolutely necessary. The Templar was the most honest and upright person I had ever encountered.

"Have a care here," he said as we approached a dark, squat dwelling with equally blackened huts on either side of it. Another time I might have bristled at the warning, but if I had learned nothing else in all of this, it was to trust in the judgment of those who knew a place or situation better than me.

We entered from the rear and moved inside with only the gray of night to light our way. The Templar advanced with confidence through an empty hallway down a set of stone stairs to a room beneath the ground.

It was blacker here than anywhere I had ever been save the cave where I had found the sacred bowl of the Holy Vessel. There I had the carving to light my way. It was not so here. This place brought my fear of dark places back to the fore of my mind. I crowded closer to the Templar than I had intended and yet he did not back me off with word or gesture as he might have in the beginning. I forced myself to give him room to move ahead and for a moment felt the trickle of nervousness rise in my throat.

The scratch of a flint and glow of a flame illuminated the space as he lit the wick of a squat candle on an old table set against the wall. We were alone in a small room without windows. Two chairs flanked the table and both were covered with clothing items. On the table were two rolled parchments sealed in deep red wax.

The Templar broke the seal on the first and nodded as he read. "Good. All is in place. Dress yerself in the clothing there, but fasten yer dagger an' sheath against yer wrist before ye do."

I eyed the pile dubiously. The clothing was like nothing I'd ever worn. On my pile were thin linen breeks, wool hose, one of blue and one of red, a shirt of pale linen, a fitted tunic of a blue, soft material I did not recognize, a dark blue hooded woolen cloak, and pointed, black leather shoes.

Quickly, I donned the shirt and tunic and swapped out my old, worn breeks with these new ones. The hose were not as simple. Though they were fitted snugly, they had to be tied to the breeks to keep them from slipping. The shoes were by far the oddest bit, tight to the sides of my feet and far longer than my toes reached, especially on the foot that was missing some. As I moved around the space, I tripped nearly every other step.

Occupied with dressing, I nearly missed seeing the Templar don the final bits of his wardrobe, but when I turned to him, I sucked in a breath in awe. Alexander looked like a King. His cloak was deep green wool on the outside and lined with the pelts of white-and-gray squirrel on the inside. The tunic beneath, barely a shade lighter and embroidered with fine threads of gold, was cut trim to his chest and fell to his feet, gathered at the waist with a gold chain belt studded with emeralds. "Ye're no' about to blend in with the commoners in that," I exclaimed.

He smiled, spread his arms wide, and dropped low in a bow. "At court, this is the only way we will blend in. Ye, on the other hand, look the part, but we have a bit o' training to do."

I almost groaned, but remembered that this was one of the very things I missed about him, his teaching. "What is my part?" I asked.

"I am a minor noble in from Scotland on my way to the northern reaches. Ye are my varlet," he said.

"And what does a varlet do?" I asked.

"Ye attend me. Prepare my clothes, fetch food from the kitchens. All o' that is o' no account when we are alone, but out in public ye must play a role that ye, my friend, might no' sit easy in."

I made to protest but he cut me off. "Ye must never raise yer eyes to any o' the aristocracy. Ye must no' speak in public, unless 'tis about the errand ye've been sent on or the meal ye are carrying."

I lapsed into silence. This might be more difficult than it seemed. "All right. No speaking. What will we be doing there?"

"Listening an' learning," he said, gathering up all of the material that was scattered across the table. I rolled our old clothes into a ball and stuffed them into my pack.

"What now?"

"We build our escort an' find a place a' court," he replied.

I followed him out the door, a bit annoyed by the information I could not seem to draw from him and by the shoes that were much too long to allow more than a hobbled step. "Head down, Tormod," Alexander said softly.

"What, why?" I asked, craning around, confused.

"Ye have to get used to the feeling before it matters." Even though there were no people around, it would seem that the pretending had begun. I dropped my gaze to the road, squared my shoulders, and nodded.

We found two horses that had been left in a small stable out back, a great black stallion for Alexander and a slightly smaller, older-looking, gray horse for me. I was not put off by the selection as it had been a while since I'd sat a horse. To have one not quite ready to take my hand off was a comfort. But as everything else I had seen of the Templar, he was a master of the horse. With very few words spoken, the prancing animal was under command and sitting still and silent beneath him.

The road seemed less frightening dressed as I was, riding such a stalwart mount. I sat straighter, keeping to my role by riding a few paces behind Alexander. It gave me time to study him. The Templar was even thinner than I had thought when I first saw him. And though he sat tall, I could see the tremor of fatigue in his back and shoulders not long into the ride.

The evening air was cold and small flakes of snow drifted down on us. The houses we passed along the road were dark and shut up tight for the night. The soft fall of the horses' hooves crackled and rattled, nearly the only sound for leagues. I knew not our destination.

But deep into the night, near on the press of morning, we rode past a wooden fence and down a lane painted white with snow to a great manor house nestled in the cup of a hillside. Beyond the shutters, candlelight flickered.

We dismounted and led our horses around the side of the house where an old man in a patched cloak met us and took them away. The Templar led the way to a door at the rear that swung open before he even had the chance to knock.

"Monsieur Alex, Gaston is gone. Please, you must find him. He's still a boy."

My heart lurched. It was Fabienne. Here. But how?

"Fabienne, I am glad that ye received my message. What is wrong?" he asked. I could feel the swirl of her worry and marveled at the quiet, intent way he was drawing the power to soothe her.

"Gaston. He left in the wake of your friends' arrival, and he has not been home since."

I drew back the hood I had pulled closed against the snow and stepped up to the door.

"You!" she shouted. "Why did you come into our lives? We've had peace. There has been no trouble for some time and I foolishly believed we were safe."

The Templar stepped between us before I could answer. "Fabienne, 'tis no' the lad's fault. Things are happening that are far beyond the three o' us. When did ye see him last?" This question was to me.

"A' the inn o' the Cochon Rouge. He left when we did, headed back toward home — or a' least that was his intention. I know, for I told him to go home myself," I said.

"Gaston's intentions are ever his own," said the Templar.

I hung my head. I was tired, and the confrontation was making me dizzy. It took a moment to realize that the Templar and Fabienne were still talking to each other, for a buzz had begun behind my eyes and my vision flickered.

"*Will ye take me to the castle?*" My heart leapt when I heard Aine's voice.

"*It is not a place that you can get into without an escort.*"

"*Well, I need to go there. I'll make it on my own. Ye need no' bother yerself.*"

"*Non, miss. My honor would not allow it. I will take you. Perhaps there is one there who we may call upon. I have friends in many places.*"

"*Gaston, who would be called 'milady' at the residence of the palace?*"

"*There are many in court that could rightfully be named such, miss.*"

"But one whose father would marry her off to the prince of a foreign land?"

"I can think of but one, miss. The Princess Isabella."

The outside of the house wavered before my eyes, and I felt the grip of the Templar bite my arms.

"He is with Aine. They head to the palace," I said softly. Fabienne gasped.

"Let us go inside," said the Templar. "The night has been long, and there is much yet to decide."

HELP FROM A FRIEND

"Have ye seen Aine a' the castle?" I asked when we were alone. Fabienne had retired and Alexander and I rested on reed mats near the hearth in her main room.

"Aye. Aine is much in my visions, but what is o' the true future an' what is o' the possible, I canno' divine. She has a role to play in much o' what is to come, either way." I closed my eyes, surprised by the sudden worry I felt. Aine was impulsive, and she was with Gaston, who was worse. Together there was no telling what trouble might befall them. I missed her, too, I realized a moment later. I had come to rely on her to quiet my fears and to enhance the scope of my visions. Now those visions were encompassing her and they were lacking in a detail that bothered me tremendously.

I remembered then a vision that had come long ago. Aine in a cloak of deep blue trimmed in the white of animal fur. Her arm had been entwined with Cornelius's. It had to have been at the palace. Where else would she be dressed in such a fine manner?

"I saw a vision o' Aine once, with Cornelius. Is it possible that he would be a' court now?" I asked.

The Templar looked thoughtful. "Aye. He is a trader. It would no' be unusual for him to be there."

I rested my head on a pile of old blankets, and my body sank into the reeds as if the mat was the finest of pallets. Exhaustion pulled at me and yet my mind was filled with too many things for sleep. Bertrand had died at the hands of the Templar trainees, of that I was sure. I wished that I had more of an understanding of the things that were going on. Perhaps if I did I might have been able to stop them.

"Tormod, sometimes ye just have to let life draw ye along. No' everything can be deciphered in an instant." His voice was soft and sure.

"But Torquil an' Aine might no' have even an instant to spare," I said, frustrated.

"Yet that possibility is no' something that ye can control," he answered. "Have faith. The Lord is watching over them, even though they are away from us."

"How can ye be assured o' that?" I said, ashamed to utter the blasphemous words.

He was quiet a moment. "We all have times when our beliefs are sorely tested, Tormod; when things happen that we wish did no', an' the sadness causes us to question our faith."

"Even ye?" I asked in a small voice.

"D'ye think me less human because I am a Templar, Tormod? I am a man just as ye. My life is no less difficult an' my trials any fewer," he said.

All at once, Fabienne's image filled my mind's eye. But just as quickly as it came, it disappeared once again. The room was dim, and I could not see the expression on his face or the look in his eyes.

"The best ye can do is say a prayer to the Lord an' do yer best to follow the way o' the light. In time yer wavering will be a thing o' the past." His belief was absolute. I felt it and knew it. Whatever it was that gave him unrest in the past, it was no longer plaguing him. Though I was curious to know, I would not ask what could have shaken the faith of one as devout as he. It was a trespass and none of my concern.

I woke to the murmur of the Templar's prayers and found warm bread and honey and a steaming mug of chamomile tea set next to me near the hearthstone. I brushed the sleep from my eyes and knelt to say my prayers, though the scent of the food made my stomach rattle.

I tucked in the moment I'd finished. My version far shorter than his, the Templar finished after my bread was long gone, and the tea was a warm memory in my gullet. The sun was creeping into the morning sky, sweeping away the dusky gray of night when he took a stool at the table to break his fast.

"We travel to the castle today, Tormod. I feel that I have to warn ye to be on yer guard. Take nothing for granted. Keep yer counsel. Speak naught but the meal, yer duties, an' possibly the weather. Trust no one outside our circle. Court is a place o' deception an' danger. The King an' his council are quick to take offense, an' even quicker to initiate punishment."

I thought his warnings a bit much, but refrained from saying so. Fabienne returned to the room then, and I drew a quick breath, stunned. It was not just the change in clothing, though that surely added to the overall effect — her robes were a vibrant blue, crusted in pearls and dripping to the rushes at her feet — but it was more the stately air she projected, as if she were born to royalty. I gaped at her, as Alexander dropped into a deep bow. "My Lady, ye're a vision o' beauty."

A faint pink dusted her cheeks. "Thank you, sir knight." She gathered a set of parchments from the table, which she folded and tucked into a pocket sewed to the inside of her cloak. "I never thought I'd return there," she said as her hands smoothed down her sides.

"I'm sorry that I had to ask ye." He stood stiffly, not meeting her eyes.

"Gaston brought this on as much as any. If" — she hesitated and caught herself — "when I see him, there will be many explanations due." Lisette then appeared with a sack that looked heavy in her small hands.

"Here, let me," I said, reaching to take it from her. She shook her head violently, and backed away as if frightened.

"It's all right, Lisette, let Tormod help. He is a friend," said Alexander.

Her pale eyes looked me over as if to judge the fact for herself. Then she handed me the bag. It was as heavy as I thought it would be. I wondered what was inside that the girl was so worried over it.

"The sooner we are on our way, the better," Alexander said, motioning Fabienne ahead of him. Lisette fell in line next and then he swept along in their wake. I trailed behind, feeling oddly left out. The snow had stopped while we slept, and now a cold mist fell. I wondered how far a ride we would have to the palace. Our horses were saddled and ready. Added to the Templar's and mine were a fine, cream palfrey for Fabienne, a small, gray pony for Lisette, and three mules laden with a variety of bags, to which I added the one I carried. Alexander helped Fabienne mount sidesaddle then stood beside his horse. "Tormod, I need ye," he said.

I was about to mount my own horse and stopped, wondering what was wrong. "Ye are my varlet, an' near court ye have to appear as such."

I scrambled to his side. "I'm sorry, I forgot." Immediately, I felt like a dolt. I didn't even know what I was supposed to do for him.

"It's all right, Tormod. No harm done. Ye've never had to do this before. I only remind ye so that it becomes more natural." He put his foot in one of the stirrups, and motioned me to his side. "Just stand before me an' allow me to put my hand on yer shoulder an' push up."

I did as he said and was surprised by the tremor that slid along his arm. I looked up at him, alarmed, but then he was in the saddle and nudging the horse forward and I had to scramble to catch up. My horse had leads to both of the mules, so there was a moment of confusion before I was able to get my train in line. By then the moment for questions had passed.

We rode in single file: Fabienne, Lisette, the Templar, and me, trekking down a lane that was more root and bramble than dirt, passing several middle-size houses scattered along the way. The estate we were leaving, the Templar had explained, was the main of several owned by Fabienne.

Missing Aine was a strange ache that clenched inside my stomach. What had she been thinking, heading off to the castle? It was ridiculous. She was like a bairn, charging in to prove that she could use the power as well as I could. I would not admit it to her, but I knew that she did. She mastered things faster. She had that knack of getting a full read of a place, while I could only receive the bits that I was granted. I snorted, annoyed with my thoughts. Lisette looked over her shoulder at me, her gaze curious.

I turned my attention to the road as we approached the branching lane where Fabienne's property ended. The mules pulled to the left, and I had to snap the lead to get them shifted and moving along with the rest of the horses to the right. When I had them on the straightaway once more, I looked over at Lisette again. She had turned her gaze back to her mistress, and hunched into the cloak she was traveling beneath. It seemed to swallow her up and hide her from the sight of any who might pass by. She was not Fabienne's child, I had learned from the Templar. She had been a servant to the Queen who had died and was left homeless when the King turned her out. Fabienne had taken her in.

The road beyond the estate was wide, and the Templar and Fabienne moved of accord to ride beside each other. I watched them absently. They were obviously long acquainted, their manner relaxed. I knew the Templar well, and I could tell that his vigilance was absolute. All the while they were speaking, his subtle draw on the power masked the whole of our contingent. I added to his efforts, working a strand of my own, and was pleased when a wash of surprise rolled between us. *Nicely done. Ye've learned much while I was away.*

I smiled in his direction. Fabienne continued to speak softly to him, and I was impressed that he didn't drop a word while we communicated. It was something I would like to work on. I wished again that Aine had not disappeared.

We rode for several marks of the candle through the countryside and approached the first of several great, wooden bridges that spanned the river to the Île de la Cité. Our horses' hooves clopped on wood ominously, and we heard the toll of a death bell ringing somewhere ahead on the island.

I knew that we were close to the grounds of the palace for the amount of people on the road grew steadily until we were fighting our way past those walking, on horse, or in wagons. My first sight of the royal grounds brought a quiver to the depths of my stomach. This was the King's domain, the powerful man behind all of the forces hunting for us. The walls rose steeply from the embankment as if they'd sprouted from the hillside. Above peered the enormity of the castle. It was grand, much larger than anything I'd ever seen before. From where I sat I could see at least ten turrets and armed guards patrolled the parapets.

There was a line waiting to enter, and we jostled our mounts into their midst. I was surprised to see the many different classes together. Some were nobly dressed as we were, but there were farmers and craftsmen as well. Lisette stared at the crowd with wide eyes, and her fright pressed at the edges of my shielding. My first reaction was to calm her, but I caught myself before drawing the power. I had to put a tight rein on myself now. I could not afford to slip up — Torquil's life might depend on it. Beneath lowered lids I took in the crowd, looking for any sign of Gaston or Aine, but found neither.

The line moved forward at a crawl, and I found myself anxious to pass through the enormous wooden gates and away from the watchful eyes of the guard. The Templar sat straight and tall in the saddle, all signs of exhaustion or weakness stripped from his demeanor. If I were a stranger, I would surely assume he was as he presented himself to be: a rich merchant, quite used to the interrogation of the King's guard.

The wind off the water was like ice against my neck and I shivered, from fear or from cold I could not tell. Voices rose ahead of us just as a large, gray wolfhound bounded to my side and circled my mount. Bran! Which meant Cornelius was near. It was all I could manage to keep the horse from balking. "Spices and pelts! That's what I declare. An' if ye know what's good for ye, ye'll be moving me along to the steward right quickly. What I bring is in demand an' the longer ye take, the higher will be my prices!" I was not sure if Bran recognizing me was a good or bad thing at the moment.

"Call yer dog to yer side," spoke the Templar in an even tone.

I looked up quickly and saw the flicker of recognition in Cornelius's eyes. A sharp whistle brought the dog obediently to the side of his master. "No offense meant, monsieur," he called, doffing his hat in a wave and moving inside without another glance.

My eyes met the Templar's, curious, and his glance darted toward the ground where my gaze was supposed to have been during the exchange. I looked down quickly. We were next in line. My heart was beating rapidly as I clucked the horse forward, trailing. "The widow dowager Lady Fabienne Letourneau," said Alexander. "An' I am Alexander MacNeil, o' the MacNeils o' Sutherland." He handed to the guard both his papers and those he had been holding for Fabienne.

"And your business?" asked the guard.

"Lies with His Highness and not with you," Fabienne said in a voice that was cold, clear, and imperious. The guard gave her no more than a cursory glance, and the whole of our company was waved inside.

The breath was tight in my chest as I passed, sure that at any moment I would be called out and tossed into the dungeons at the whim of the King. But it seemed this fate was not to be.

We passed through a large courtyard, several great halls, and up a stairwell to the second floor. Here we parted ways with Fabienne and Lisette. They were to stay in the opposite wing beneath the former rooms of the late Queen Joan, adjoining the suite of the Royal Princess. The memory of her image came swiftly to mind as I watched them walk away, and I wondered idly if I might see her during our stay.

The thought was immediately squashed when the Templar called me to his side to carry his bags. I was a varlet. There would be no royalty for me. Though I surely had no wish to meet the King, the Princess was another matter entirely.

The Templar and I were to be housed with the rest of the courtiers beneath the apartments of the King, in a place I hoped Cornelius also stayed. The corridor was long and appointed richly with tapestries lining the walls and statues on tables scattered between the many-banded wooden doors. Guards were stationed at each end of the hall, and servants moved with purpose in and out of the rooms. The Templar stopped at a door near the stairs and waited. I stood behind him wondering what was keeping him from entering. He looked at me pointedly, and I realized my mistake. Quickly, I hurried to the door and opened it inward, stepping back so he could enter. Without further pause, he swept inside. I took a quick look around and moved in behind him, breathing deeply once I had closed the door.

"What's a dowager?" I asked, remembering the title he had bestowed on Fabienne.

" 'Tis a widow who has inherited property from her husband. Fabienne has estates in several places up north. One of the reasons she did no' wish to return to court is that many of the lesser nobles, the ones who do no' have land or funds of their own, will be inclined to press for her hand." As he spoke he seemed to be staring off into nothingness, but his features looked clouded with regret.

"But wouldn't getting married be a good thing? Isn't that what all women want?" I dropped our bags and began to unpack his.

"Don't take out my mantle or anything that would mark me as a Templar," he said. "Just put it all in the wardrobe a' the bottom. We'll be seeing the seamstress shortly to outfit ourselves." He dropped to a sturdy chair in the corner and took out his papers, laying them on the table. "No. No' every woman wants to be married. Especially to someone chosen by the King, sold off as a favor to pay one o' his many debts. Fabienne runs her estates. She genuinely cares for her tenants, an' her people adore her. A King's man would put all that she loves in jeopardy," he said.

I wondered then why she would do this, bring us here and pave the way for our stay at the castle, but I remembered that Gaston was here. Still she could have sent someone ahead to call him home. My eyes rested on the tall, elegant knight before me and in an instant, I knew the answer. It was written in the lines of his face and the expression on hers whenever I saw them together. Fabienne was in love with the Templar Alexander.

The thought stunned me. There was no future there.

He was a man of the cloth — he would never be allowed to marry her. I snuck a look at him from the corner of my eye. Did he love her as well?

"Best begin finding yer way around, Tormod. I need ye to make arrangements for the seamstress, get me some parchment, ink, and quills, an' then fetch us some food from the kitchens. We've missed the noon repast, an' dinner will no' be for some time. I need to do some correspondence. Ask the guard at the end o' the hall for directions an' remember to keep yer head down. Stay as small as the mice that wander these halls for we must, above all, no' be recognized."

A REUNION OF SORTS

I let myself out of our chambers with the sound of the Templar's prayers a soft murmur behind me. Mindful of all he said, I tried to keep my eyes as much to the floor as was possible without walking into something. I was glad for the dye that still tinted my hair, for in this place I saw no one with carrot red hair.

I followed the corridor, watching and listening for signs of Cornelius, but for once, if the man was present he was silent. A guard by the stairs gave me directions to the kitchens, and I took the winding staircase down to the main floor. Being here, so close to where Torquil was said to be held, was torture. The temptation to reach for him using the power ate at my resolve with every footfall. Only the thought of Gaylen and the possibility of other gifted stayed me.

The kitchens were on the main floor but tucked away behind a maze of narrow corridors that were dark but for the few rush torches that gave off a dim glow. It was odd to bear the full brunt of attention that was focused on me the moment the doors opened beneath my touch. Inside was an assortment of workers, clothed in the drab homespun that was much more familiar to me than the finery of the day.

"*Oui*, milord. Is there something you require?" The query was asked of me from a woman whose broad girth, muscled arms, and red face proclaimed her mistress of the premises.

I was startled by the title she gave me, but realized that most likely any servant of a lord was of a birth higher than any here. "Bread, an' perhaps some meat, if ye will. For . . ." I hesitated, nearly undone by the pretense. "Lord Alexander MacNeil."

"He's the new one. Came in with the Lady Fabienne," someone whispered. I turned toward the voice only to encounter the dipped heads of several of the kitchen maidens.

"Ah, I've heard about that one," someone else murmured.

"Shush!" warned the mistress harshly. Not another word came from them. "Pay them no mind, if you would, milord. They mean no harm." She bustled toward me and put a dark loaf of bread, a large wedge of cheese, a packet of some type of meat, and a pitcher of ale in my overloaded hands. I nodded and turned to leave. From behind came another whisper. "He's lovely."

My ears burned as I pushed beyond the doors back into the cool of the darkened corridor. The lasses were different here than at home. I remembered at the last moment that I had forgotten to ask about the seamstress and turned back inside. "I beg pardon, mistress," I began, but the swing of the door from the opposite side of the room caught my attention like a rabbit in a snare.

A pair of frozen gray eyes seized upon mine, and my heart surged within my chest. Gaston! A subtle shake of his head brought me to my senses just as I would have blurted out our acquaintance.

"*Oui,* milord. Is there something else?" asked the mistress.

"Oh, aye. A seamstress. Where can I find one?"

"Willy will send one up to you. Where can he tell them to go?"

"The suite o' the Lord MacNeil on the second tier, madame."

"We will send the word, milord." She hovered near a table, clearly held up by my slowly departing self. I glanced quickly at Gaston and turned on my heels.

A SERVANT TO ROYALTY

"How could ye bring her here?!" I railed at Gaston, who had appeared within the candle mark at the suite of the Templar.

"Keep yer voice down, Tormod," the Templar warned. "The castle has ears in all places."

"Where is she, Gaston?" I demanded, albeit a bit more quietly. Everything within me wanted to bolt down the hallways banging on doors until I found her.

"Aine is in the employ of the Princess," he said somewhat reluctantly.

I gasped and even the Templar appeared shocked by the news. "How is that possible? Gaston, what have ye done?" The Templar's tone was low and steady, but I knew that voice. Gaston had better have a very good answer.

"She was determined, Monsieur Alex. If I didn't help, she would have tried to do it on her own somehow."

"Tell me now," he said.

"I followed Tormod and Aine to the inn when they left the Cochon Rouge. I knew that they would have need of my services and mamere was already angry with me, so I thought it would be better if I gave her a little time to cool."

"She is no' cool, Gaston. She is worried an' she is here," the Templar said.

Gaston turned paler than the white of his skin seemed capable. He shook his head and began to pace. "The mistress was most distressed when I arrived. Tormod had taken his pack and gone off, and she was at the inn alone." He shot me a dirty look, which I at once took offense to. "She said that she must get to the palace and find the Princess. Though she would not tell me why, she was insistent. I thought perhaps she imagined that you had come here without her."

"That's ridiculous. I left her to find Bertrand. I had every intention o' returning to the inn. Where is she now?"

"In the chambers of the Princess," he said calmly. "I arranged for her position. She is my cousin Robert from my father's lands to the west." He seemed proud to have been of help.

"Yer cousin? A lad?" I asked, incredulous. "No one will believe that for a moment."

"But they already do," he said. "She is a favorite of the Princess."

"This is a strange turn o' events," said the Templar. "Why would she do something like this?"

I told him then about the vision of the Princess that Aine and I had shared, then paced the room like a tethered animal. "We've got to get her out o' there before she ruins our chance to save Torquil."

"There is little hope of that. The Princess seems a bit taken by her," Gaston said.

"Ye jest," I scoffed. "Taken, as in attracted to her, as a lad?"

Gaston grinned and shrugged his shoulders.

The thought took a moment to sink in, then I found it oddly humorous as well. How could that possibly be in Aine's plans? Gaston's grin was contagious.

"This may actually work to our advantage," said the Templar. "Can ye get a message to her, Gaston?"

"Aye. I work in the kitchen, and she has been assigned to carry up the meals of the Princess."

"Good. I want ye to tell her to meet us in Cornelius's room tonight after dinner. He is in the west wing o' this floor. The Princess will retire with her ladies to her solar. Aine, naturally, will no' be allowed to join them. She will have to return the cups an' platters to the kitchen an' so will be able to slip away for a short while."

Gaston nodded. "I'd better get back — the kitchens are very busy. The Holy Father is due to stop here on his way to Avignon. The preparations are underway for the feast in his honor."

"Ye will no' long be in the kitchens, Gaston, when yer mamere finds ye," said the Templar.

Gaston stared at the Templar boldly. "Do not tell her that you have seen me," he said. "I am the only contact with Aine that you have." He ducked out the door before the Templar could reply, my shocked gaze following.

Bran laid his furry head on my lap, his deep brown eyes asking, *Where is she?* The answer was one I could only guess at, though I shared his eagerness to know. The Templar and I had taken our meal in Cornelius's suite, a set of rooms far more elaborate than our own. "Have ye any word o' the arrival o' prisoners?" the Templar asked.

Cornelius sat in an ornate chair before a roaring fire. My feet were outstretched as I sat on a stool nearby, taking advantage of the heat that was not present in many of the rooms of this dark castle. That the Templar and Cornelius were long acquaintances was a surprise to me and yet it made sense, because they moved in similar circles. Alexander was an envoy to the English court, representing the Templars on home soil. Cornelius traded with many courts — French, English, and Spanish alike.

" 'Tis said that there is one on the way who is quite valuable. No' much has been spoken, but I have a man in the dungeon guard with a particular taste for a spice I bring from the east. The prisoner he said is to arrive with the guard o' the Holy Father."

"That canno' be Torquil, then," I said. "Why would he be anywhere near the guard o' His Holiness?" I turned to the Templar. "Ye said he was on a ship destined for here."

"I said that he was on a ship headed this way. He could have as easily been taken to Rome, though I have had no visions that have showed him to be there. Cornelius, did the guard say anything o' a newly come young prisoner here?" he asked.

Cornelius's gaze rested on me kindly, weighing his words. "He patrols only the upper dungeons an' has spoken o' no one that matches the description."

"But," I prompted. He was obviously holding something back.

"But I've no' posed that question directly, an' there are two levels beneath those rooms. Levels for those who have no currency to barter for better." He stood and busied himself with a group of bags in the corner. I swallowed hard.

"We've got to get down there," I said.

"Plans are already in place. Ye will be best served on the sidelines, Tormod." The Templar was reading a small stack of documents that had been delivered from Fabienne. I felt stifled, not being allowed to do anything to help our cause or even to know what plans the Templar was moving ahead with. When I had prodded him earlier, he had said that it was best that I did not know all, that too much information in too many hands right now was dangerous. I was annoyed. This was my brother we were talking about, and I was the chosen Protector of the Holy Vessel.

"I'll take back the platters," I mumbled.

The Templar did not look up from his reading. "Do no' go anywhere or do anything more than that, Tormod." My face flamed. To be reprimanded before Cornelius was mortally difficult to take.

With arms laden, I nudged aside the door, careful to give away nothing of my thoughts, and nearly dropped the load. "Aine . . ." I began, flustered and glad to see her at the same time. She was dressed as a servant boy in tight breeks and a short, linen tunic. "Thank the Lord yer safe." My honest and heartfelt words fell into dead air.

"Tormod." The chill in her tone brought my anger with her to the surface.

"Why did ye leave?" I snapped.

She gaped at me, her eyes flashing and her cheeks growing red. "*Ye* left *me* there, Tormod. Without a word o' explanation!"

My heart twisted. She didn't know about Bertrand. How could I tell her? Before I could gather a thought she pushed past, and as her arm swung it brushed my own. Anger and hurt swirled through her to me, but also the peace she always managed to project, soothed the ragged places within. I wanted to reach out, to stop her and explain, but the words were not clear and she was already into the suite. I followed her inside and closed the door behind.

All eyes had turned toward her, but the first to react was Bran, who launched himself across the room, planted his paws on her chest, and began earnestly lapping her face. "Bran, ye big dolt. Get yerself off the lass," said Cornelius, whose face mirrored the pleasure of his dog at her arrival. "It's good to see ye, little miss," he said gruffly.

She laughed and the sound made me oddly joyful inside. I had missed her, though the time had not been overly long. "And ye must be the Templar, Alexander," she said a bit shyly.

He stood and approached her quietly. "'Tis good to meet a' last." His smile was deep and welcoming, and something inside me twisted. "Ye have advanced our endeavors greatly an' I thank ye."

"'Tis ye we must thank. Had ye no' enhanced our reach an' been within range o' Tormod's brother, perhaps this day would tell another tale."

"We have all done our part," he replied. "A part that is far from finished. Come, ye will have little enough time among us. The Princess will be seeking ye soon."

Aine seated herself on a wooden bench on a raised carpeted dais by the fire. The Templar and Cornelius joined her there. I stayed behind and watched as Bran arranged himself at her feet. I felt oddly apart from them.

"I canno' say that I approve o' the dangerous position ye've set yerself in, but if God wills it, it will be a boon to us," Alexander continued. "The Princess is able to move about the castle with more freedom than any other within these walls. An' she is often to be found in the royal library. There is something there that I need for ye to seek out, Aine."

"She canno' read," I said plainly. "What good would it be to have her nose about the library?" I hadn't meant to sting her, but I had done it nonetheless. Her face flamed, and her eyes darkened with anger.

" 'Tis no' something written on a page, but rather an object hidden somewhere in the stacks. I have seen the library an' had visions o' the King standing by the shelves nearest the windows. He takes something out of a darkened space an' stares at it greedily, often. I need to know what 'tis." The Templar was entrusting Aine with a secret duty that by rights should have come to me.

"But how will I know what to look for? An' how will I manage with the Princess an' all o' the guards standing by?" she asked.

"I don't actually want ye to seek it out. I want ye to read the room an' tell me what this thing is."

"Aye. I can do that," she said eagerly.

I grimaced. She could do that, and it was something that I, likely, could not. The thought didn't sit well.

"How d'ye fare? Are there any in the Princess's employ who are questioning yer position?" the Templar asked.

"There is one I am uncomfortable around. 'Tis the King's man, de Nogaret. I feel him watching me, like a hawk about to kill, but I don't think 'tis because he recognizes me. I don't know what he wants." She shivered at whatever thought rippled through her, and I knew suddenly that she was thinking about her uncle. She knew more than she was saying, and it frightened me. I had to get her alone and find out what it was she was holding back.

"Stay as far from him as ye can. For yer safety as well as yer position. It would take nothing for him to dismiss ye," said the Templar. "Ye'd best be gone now before ye are found to be missing."

Aine nodded, gave one last pet to Bran, and stood. "I will come to ye when I can," she said, moving toward the door. My eyes followed her path and just before she passed beyond she looked back at me. *I'm sorry.* I spoke the words mentally without thinking about the price.

"Tormod," the Templar snapped in warning. I broke the link quickly and apologized. Any mindspeech was dangerous. I knew that. When I turned back toward the door, Aine was gone.

COURTLY ENDEAVORS

Sleep was a long time coming and I woke early, too keyed up to rest. Strange dreams of Gaylen and the carving took up much of the night. I saw him holding it aloft and calling upon it, but I had the feel that it was not behaving the way he wanted it to. His frustration followed me into the day, leaving me particularly edgy and raw.

All about the castle, workers moved at a feverish pitch. Word had reached us that the Holy Father had arrived during the night, and the King had called for a session of the courts to be held following the morning meal. The Templar and I took great care in dressing in the new wardrobe that had arrived from the seamstress. My hands shook as I went about my duties, and the Templar reached out to still them. "Take a deep breath, Tormod, an' let the power center ye. What will come o' the day, will."

The words were simple. If only the task were as well. A session of the courts might involve Torquil. When at last we were finished, I stood by the door waiting as the Templar tucked several small knives into sheathes at his wrists and hip. "Can I . . ." I began.

"If ye are found with weapons, ye will be put immediately into the dungeon an' it would take more connections than I have to free ye."

It was a harsh sentiment, but I would do nothing to jeopardize Torquil's life. I swept before him and stood at the door. "Are ye ready, my lord?" I asked. At his nod, I opened the door and gestured him to proceed. He inclined his head as he passed and I followed close at his heels.

In the hallway were a number of nobles and servants making their way toward the stairwell. As we joined them, I felt the eyes of the curious slide over us, but when I raised my gaze no one was looking, just a glance or the turn of a head, timed to avoid being caught. The Templar cleared his throat, and I jerked my eyes downward.

The floor below teemed with activity. An enormous hall was set up with row after row of long tables lined with benches and filled with people eating, drinking, and talking. High, long windows brought sunlight streaming down on the servants, who moved quickly and ably through the narrow aisles around the tables, filling trenchers and goblets the moment they were empty. Highborn and peasant alike ate together.

The Templar took a seat on the bench, and I hung back to see what I should do next. He motioned to the bench and I dropped beside him. "Can I fetch ye anything, my lord?" I asked quietly.

"I thank ye, lad, but the kitchen staff will see to it that we break our fast. Eat quickly, there are many to move in an' out o' here before court is taken up for the day. An' we will need to secure a place near Fabienne."

I looked around. It seemed a fair informal room for something like court. "They will hear the cases in this place?" I asked.

He nodded. A servant dropped bowls of a warm grain porridge and loaves of newly baked bread for each of us. Honey and almond paste followed with a steaming brew of a leaf I was unfamiliar with. If this were the meal offered every day, it was no wonder the room was bursting with people. Still I wondered how it was that the lowborn were allowed inside and asked.

"It has been a long-standing tradition with the French court that all are welcome inside the castle. It shows the magnanimity o' the King for all his people." I nodded and busied myself with eating.

Out of the corner of my eye, I saw Fabienne approach with Lisette trailing close behind. The Templar stood and I quickly did as well. "Join us, please, my Lady," he said. And she dropped down beside me, across from him.

"It is said that the Archbishop Lambert travels with His Holiness, and that the prisoner they bring comes from the Isles of Scotia," Fabienne said. I sucked in a breath. Torquil. What was I to do?

"No matter what is said here today, Tormod, ye will stay silent an' react no' at all. If 'tis something ye do no' think ye can manage, ye should wait in the suite until I come back for ye." His words were spoken softly, but it was as if he had shouted them into my face. I blinked and looked quickly around, then ducked my head.

"No. I will be all right. I need to be here," I mumbled. The food was not a draw for me anymore. I pushed my portion away and offered my bread to Lisette, who took it with somber, fearful eyes. I wondered what would put such a look into the gaze of a child.

Even before Fabienne and Lisette had finished, the benches and tables were being pushed to the outer edges of the room and an elaborate dais flanked by one highly ornamented chair was carried in from another room. The number of guards around the chamber was suddenly far more than it had been just moments before, and everything within me stilled.

I craned around a group of crofters who had suddenly pushed forward. A ripple of excitement passed through the crowd, and the doors were drawn wide as a procession of richly dressed women swept in by twos to the sound of the royal trumpets. Up the aisle and through the benches they moved as if they were not walking, but floating. And then alone she came.

Her hair was bound in a chain of gold net that sparkled in the gleam of the sunlight. Her dress was the color of rubies and her skin as pale as the first snow of winter. But it was her eyes that drew me most. Amber and gold, like the rippling water of the burns rushing over the rocks of my homeland, fringed by lashes of deep thick brown. I stared as her head turned in my direction, latched on to my gaze, and held.

A sharp elbow dug into my side, and I was pulled roughly away. The intrusion was a surprise and yet the absolute balm that washed through me at her touch stalled my indignant reply. "Are ye no' supposed to be about yer duties?" I asked, masking my pleasure at Aine's appearance.

"In here she has only women," she replied. I quickly glanced about the chamber. "She is protected, fear no'. There are guards all about the crowd to ensure it." Aine's shields were thin and I felt her swirl of annoyance, though I did not know what it was she was off about.

"Aine, there's something ye should know." I had been thinking of Bertrand for much of the night, and my chest ached with the knowledge that I would have to be the one to tell her. She turned to me expectantly, and I lowered my shields and called the painful memory to the fore, careful to mask the ripple.

Aine's gasp and the quick bite of her grip on my arm was covered by the arrival of the King's company. "Kneel," I urged, and drew her down even as I felt the surge of sadness churn inside her. Tears were better concealed with a crowd focused elsewhere. Her body shook.

"That's why ye left," she whispered. I nodded, barely able to contain my own sorrow. I had pushed it away to someplace deep inside of me, but with Aine here, it bubbled back up to the surface.

"But why?" Her words shook as she fought for control. "I don't understand." The rustle of the crowd as the King took his place on the dais covered only a moment of conversation.

" 'Twas the trainees, though I know no' why," I murmured.

"No more now," said the Templar softly. "There will be time to talk later. Aine, go to Cornelius's suite. He waits for ye there."

She ducked her head and took her leave. The absent feel of her hand on my arm was nearly painful. The Templar moved beside me as the King called, "Bring in the petitioners." I looked up at him for the first time, this man whom I had feared for so long. He was large and strong, with a long, angular face whose eyes stared ahead as if he were both here and somewhere else as well, as if his mind were not wholly in this room. His waving brown hair fell to his shoulders, and the great golden crown, set with a multitude of jewels, glistened in the morning light. Blue silk draped to the floor in a pool of light, and he was as still as one of the many statues that circled the great courtyard outside.

The doors at the end of the hall creaked as they were drawn wide once more, and everyone turned toward the sound. A procession of brown-robed monks, softly singing their prayers, entered first. Then followed a group of priests in shades of black and red — bishops, archbishops, and cardinals. As the first of the ranks moved up the aisle, the inhabitants of the hall once again dropped to their knees, crossed themselves, and praised the Lord. I followed their example, staring raptly as each passed, waiting with my breath held tight in my chest. And then he came. The Holy Father nearly glowed in the brilliant red of his vestments. His pale skin and almost paler eyes were such a sharp contrast to the robes, almost as if he were a living flame. I blinked as the vision washed over me. White robes. Red flame. Smoke. Pain. Blistering agony.

The Templar's hand was on the nape of my neck pressing down, his whisper deep in my head. *Let it go. Quickly.* The room swam into focus and yet the memory of the pain in my feet made me near faint. The Holy Father's procession was done, and all of the conclave were seated to the right hand of the King.

"Let the petitioners begin," called the King. And so it began. I had never been present at the judgments by our laird and so stood, rapt, as case after case was brought before the assembled. Some were as simple as the theft of a cow. Others more difficult, with each side shouting and demanding that justice, whatever justice was seen fit by the King, was acted upon. The candle marks crept by and the cases began to seem less and less real and important. Until there came one prisoner.

He was beaten and bloody, fouled with the dirt of a long imprisonment. His face barely recognizable, and yet my heart went still at the sight of him. The Abbot stood in the center of the hall, wavering on his feet as the charges rang out. Obstruction. Tax evasion. Blasphemy. The list did not sound as though any of it were truly horrible, until the last charge was read. Murder.

I started forward, but the Templar tightly held me back. What I had planned to do, I had no idea, but I felt as though a terrible wrong was being enacted and I was compelled to stop it. The Abbot could not have committed murder. It was not in the man I knew.

"Mercy, my Lord. Please, for the sake o' one of God's chosen." The Archbishop Lambert, Alexander's friend, spoke the words. I hadn't recognized him in the long procession but now was grateful for his presence.

"The law is not only for the ordinary man, Your Grace. It does not recognize the trappings of faith. Only what is proven and right, and in enforcing the law we praise His name." He stared at the man, who dropped suddenly to his knees, unable to bear his own weight on shaking legs. "Hang him!"

The porridge I'd eaten surged to my throat, and I clapped my hand to my mouth to keep it down. The noise of the crowd was deafening, and I stood helplessly as soldiers of the King dragged the Abbot out of the hall. "Canno' ye do anything?" I whispered furiously to the Templar.

"No' here, Tormod. Let us be gone."

CROSS PURPOSES

We found Aine in the suite of Cornelius with a fine blue silken dress draped over her arm. I remembered the vision from a long time past of Aine in this very dress with a fine cloak of white fur and her hand on the sleeve of Cornelius, but something was different. In that vision, Aine's hair was not the short cap of curls that it was right now. A rope of braid had circled her head and in it was woven jewels and pearls.

"There must be something we can do," Cornelius said, pacing. "Clearly the Grand Master knows nothing about this, else he would be here demanding that the Abbot be set free. The Abbot canno' be brought up on charges of tax evasion. He is a part of the Order, an' the Order is exempt from any an' all taxes."

"The charges are a farce," said the Templar. "Something made up to get the Abbot out of the way. But for what?"

"What could an unknown abbot from a small preceptory in Scotland mean to the King of France?" Aine asked, catching my eye, but looking away just as quickly. .

"He is no' unknown, nor insignificant," said the Templar. "He is the single most important money handler in the whole o' the Templar Order. I do no' think his abduction was by chance. But the why o' it still eludes me."

"What can we do?" I asked.

"I've sent a man to the preceptory to deliver a message to the Grand Master," he said.

"But there are those within who work a' cross purposes," said Aine. "They've killed Bertrand. Is it someone who can be trusted?"

"Aye," he replied. "The Archbishop can gain entrance an' a private audience as no other would be able."

"But what are we to do in the meantime? We are still no closer to finding out where Torquil is," I said.

Seeing the state of the Abbot had built a knot in the pit of my stomach that refused to go away.

"Aine, have ye had any progress in getting inside the library?" the Templar asked.

"Aye. We were there this morning. It seems that the Princess has a great love for the room. Her mother had the place filled, an' she has read nearly everything on the shelves," she said.

"Truly?" I said, unable to keep the surprise from my tone. "She can read?" Aine narrowed her eyes, then ignored me.

"There are so many memories in that room that I could not sort out the ones ye're needing. I'll try again as soon as I might," she said.

"I'm not altogether comfortable with ye staying with the Princess. One more day an' then we must give up on that tack. Ye will join Cornelius a' the evening meal tomorrow as his newly arrived niece from Scotland."

"But her hair —" I began.

"What the devil is wrong with my hair, Tormod?" Aine was angry with me and as usual I could not understand why.

" 'Tis just that 'tis short, an' all the ladies here wear it long," I fumbled with my words as the image of the Princess came to mind.

"Fabienne can provide a veil. I will have her meet ye here," the Templar said.

Everyone, it seemed, had a duty in this but me. But I had more to think on right now. I moved toward the window as the conversation continued without me. I looked out to the river where boats bobbed sluggishly in the early afternoon light. The sound of the wind whipping against the castle countered my restlessness and the despair that was starting to eat away at me. In my ears came a sudden keening and my eyesight faded. A thick, iron ring pounded deep into the wall. A length of chain looped through it and attached to heavy manacles. Wrists cut and burning. The dirt wet with sweat and urine. The dark deep and the smell strong. Blood.

"What d'ye see?" Aine's hand on my back drew me from the vision.

"We've got to get him out o' there," I murmured.

"Who?" she asked as I gripped the window edges.

"I don't know. The Abbot. Torquil. Me, mayhap." My heart was heavy. The Abbot was surely in the dungeons. Torquil might be there as well. And we were standing around without a plan to rescue them. If I had the carving I could use the power to tear down the walls and take them out of there. If I hadn't lost it to Gaylen.

"There is time, Tormod. We will find him." Her hand was still on my back, and I felt her determination and support. At all times, Aine's touch stilled the unrest within me, but I moved from her reach and stood alone. I didn't want comfort right now. I wanted to feel the anger and despair rolling through me. Deep beneath the base of the castle, the power of the land churned.

The Templar raised his eyes from the documents he was looking over. "Tormod. Triple shield." The censure was there in his tone. I blinked, realizing that my moods were rippling the power and drew the shields tight around me. I turned back toward the window, and Aine moved off for the door.

"I'd best be going," she said. "The Princess will be finishing her prayers."

"Good evening to ye, then, miss," said Cornelius. "Bran an' I will wait for ye on the morrow."

I turned back only to see her slip beyond the door.

"We've got to get down to the dungeons," I said quietly.

"We must bide our time, Tormod. The King is a man who must be moved politically. This dungeon is no' like the one ye liberated me from. 'Tis heavily guarded, an' ye must remember that there is still a price on our heads." He stood and secured the documents in his cloak. "Let us retire. I will need ye to deliver a message to the suite o' the Archbishop."

"Cornelius, Lady Fabienne will be dining with us tonight. Would ye make the arrangements?" he asked.

"Aye. I will, Alexander."

DELIVERY AND DISCOVERY

I passed through the halls as if I were shadow, drawing my shielding around me, using only the faintest of power to mask my presence. The suite of the Archbishop, the Holy Father, and his conclave were situated in the wing that housed the King. Security was on high alert, and I was frightened. The parchments I carried tucked away in my chausses were treasonous. At each of the checkpoints, armed guards stood at attention. Only the forged papers provided by Alexander and Fabienne's contacts allowed me to move through each as if I belonged. When at long last I arrived at the Archbishop's suite, a trickle of sweat ran down my back.

"The Archbishop is with another at the moment, but if you would like to wait here, he will see you shortly thereafter." A soft-spoken priest in a plain linen robe motioned me onward.

I took a seat on a hard wooden bench in the hallway outside his chamber. The light was dim and I was fairly hidden, but still the squeal of the door made me start. I ducked my head as two soldiers passed without a glance. A moment later, the Archbishop appeared. "Come in, lad," he said, without speaking my name. Only when the doors closed behind us did I dare to breathe.

"Yer Grace," I said, dropping to one knee and kissing his ring.

"Tormod, 'tis very good to see ye alive an' well. I feared for ye when I heard o' the warrants posted in Edinburgh. Tell me what has happened."

"Thank ye, Yer Grace." I was afraid to speak. The Templar had warned me that the castle had many eyes and ears, and this suite was less than secure with so many guards and servants about.

"The Templar asked me to give ye these. They will explain better than I have the ability." I looked quickly about, anxious to leave. But the Archbishop was not ready to release me.

"I thank ye for yer delivery," he said, taking the papers and moving to the light. "Ye have done much o' that these past months?"

I wasn't following. "Beg pardon, Yer Grace?"

"Delivering. Ye delivered a very special package a short while ago to the Abbot, did ye not, Tormod?" he asked. "'Tis such a terrible situation, his incarceration. I wanted to make sure that delivery arrived safely before he was arrested."

He was talking about the Holy Vessel. "Och, aye, Yer Grace, it was delivered with all haste." I hesitated, and he raised his snowy eyebrows.

"There have been difficulties in that matter," I said, looking pointedly at the door where outside a guard stood in attendance.

"Oh?" he asked. "What difficulties?"

I wanted to shout at his ignorance of my discomfort. "A bit o' what was delivered was then taken," I hedged.

"Come now, lad, be plain with me," he said, looking expectantly at me.

The sweat was dripping down my neck as I fought to come up with words suitable and yet vague enough that anyone listening would be left behind. "Some o' my delivery rests safely at its destination an' some o' it lies with one whom it should not. Yer Grace, perhaps it would be best if ye spent some time with . . ." I hesitated, not even wanting to use his title here where we were still outlawed. "Alexander. I am sure all o' yer questions will have answers."

He appeared disappointed. "As ye wish, then, lad."

I was relieved. "Thank ye, Yer Grace, I'd best be getting back now."

He nodded and as I hurried out of the suite, I heard him break the wax seal on the papers I'd left.

The corridor beyond the guard was curiously empty. And though I was in a hurry to be away from the Archbishop, something within me suggested that I move slowly through this part of the castle. At the first bend in the corridor, I heard feet approaching and I ducked through an unlatched door off to my left. With my ear pressed against the wood I listened as the muffled footsteps moved past. Then without warning tightness slid through my limbs and I suddenly felt as if I could not move. Within me longing stretched and clawed and I grasped the door to keep from rushing out of the room. Gaylen, here in the castle with the carving. How? Why? Did he know that we were here? Had he told de Nogaret, and did the King now realize that the quarry he sought was under his very roof? My breath was short as the power beneath the castle began to rise under my feet. Frantic, I pressed it back down, reinforcing my shielding as fast as I could, worried that Gaylen would sense it and all would be lost. I had to get word to the Templar Alexander and find Aine.

Beyond the door, the footsteps in the corridor grew fainter. Gaylen's men had turned into a room somewhere ahead. I lingered behind only a moment to be sure he wouldn't return for me, then edged into the empty hall. The clink of armor rang from beyond the bend, and I moved with purpose and kept my eyes firmly on the stones at my feet. The King's guard passed without a glance.

DESPERATE DISOBEDIENCE

"We need to find Torquil an' get out o' this castle," I said breathlessly. "Gaylen is here an' he can recognize both Aine an' myself, even if no others can."

The Templar paced slowly, his face a grave mask. "This is a complication. We need to stay an' parlay for the release o' the Abbot, an' find out about Torquil, but 'tis true that neither o' ye can afford to be seen." He turned to me. "Ye will limit yerself to the suite, until we can establish how long he intends to remain."

"No. Ye need me," I protested.

"Tormod, he is up to something, o' that we are all certain. But in this ye canno' be a part. This thing is no' just about you or me, Tormod. 'Tis about the Holy Vessel — what 'tis trying to tell us an' why it has come back into the world after all this time."

I knew that he was right in that. I had been thinking along those paths for the last moon or more, but he was wrong as well. I was a large part of this. The carving chose me, for whatever the reason. Confined to the suite I could do nothing to establish what that reason was or to get it back. My face gave me away as usual.

"All o' this is larger an' more important than we few individuals. We must place eyes an' ears within the King's complement. We've got to find out who he is meeting with an' what they are talking about." He moved to the door, and I went to follow.

"No, Tormod. Stay." He passed through the door and out of sight before I could protest. His words were to me as if I were a hound. Sit and stay. I thought of Aine moving unaware of Gaylen's presence within the chambers of the Princess. She had to be warned. I could not heed his command this time.

There were many guards stationed in the corridors that led to the wing of the Princess. I carried a tray laden with the afternoon repast that I had pilfered from the kitchen, with Gaston's help. I moved with steady purpose and found that none stopped my progress with either word or look. The halls were dim and nearly empty of passersby. The King's court session had resumed for the afternoon and most of the castle had returned to the great hall to either watch or participate.

When I'd sought out Gaston, he told me that the Princess had retired to her chambers and that she did not intend to reappear before the evening meal. A message had come from the English King: The Church had blessed the suit of his son as her future husband. The Princess was in a rare fury.

"A tray for the Princess," I said to the guard who stood outside the door of her rooms. "I was told to bring it quickly."

"I will not do it!" The raised voice was accompanied by the crash of something fragile against the back of the large wooden door. The guard flinched.

"Better you than I," he said with a grimace. "Watch your head as you enter."

He opened the door a hair and another crash sent shards of a pot tumbling into the corridor. I ducked inside to find Aine doing her best to keep the Princess from turning the suite on end, moving breakable items from her path and generally scrambling about while the maidservants stood by, wringing their hands and burying their heads in their aprons.

"Yer tray, my Lady," I said, dodging a silk-ribboned slipper that flew over my shoulder.

"Who are you, and what are you doing here?" the Princess demanded. "You are not our servant!" She had paused in the middle of her tirade to look me over. I met her eyes with innocence.

"Gaston was called upon by yer royal father to take a meal to His Holiness. I am fulfilling his duties," I said.

My voice seemed to take her aback. "Where are you from? You speak strangely." She moved closer, and I was ensnared by the color and fire in her eyes. I had seen them in the vision and had met them as she entered the great hall only this morning. Up close they were even more magnificent. I could not seem to form a thought for a moment.

Aine, who had been cleaning up the mess, passed by me, snapping a linen as if to shake it out very near the edge of my tray. I turned and narrowed my eyes at her. She moved on as if the slight was unintended.

"I am from Scotia, my Lady. Come with a group o' traders seeking work for the winter in the kitchens." I remembered that servants would not meet the Princess's eyes so I focused on the floor, trying my best to look meek.

"Scotia? Is that not a part of that horrible land they call England?" she demanded. Even from my vantage I could see her fisted hands and the tautness of her posture.

"'Tis, an' is no' as well, my Lady. Scotia is its own land, an' its people are fighting the English for their independence," I explained. "The crowned King is Robert the Bruce, although the English King does no' honor the title."

"The English King," she scoffed. "My soon to be father-in-law." She took a quick hold of the pitcher on my tray before Aine could stop her and threw it full force at the stone wall to the right of the door frame.

"My Lady, you must calm yerself. It will do you no good to allow the world to see you at your worst," said one of her ladies. "You're a princess and someday you will be the Queen of England."

This seemed to infuriate her more than appease her. I steadied the tray and moved it subtly when she would have snatched the plate and sent it flying as well. Unfortunately, my movement put her a bit off balance and I was forced to drop the tray and catch the Princess before she stumbled. The plate of meat and cheese and the bowl of stew landed in a heap on the fine carpet and the Princess in a sprawl against my chest. Her surprised wide eyes met mine and my arms closed tight around her back so that she would not fall into the mess. Her face was pink, close, and lovely, and the faint scent of lavender hung on her breath.

I sidestepped us both around the mess and helped her to stand while Aine stared in horrified fascination. "You may release me now," she said a bit breathlessly, and I realized I had quite forgotten that my arms were still around her.

"Aye. O' course," I mumbled, stepping away and stooping to stack what I could back on the tray. Aine knelt beside me.

"What the devil are ye doing here, Tormod?" Her whisper was fierce.

"Gaylen is in the castle," I murmured as I hurriedly hefted the tray. Aine's heart had begun to race. I felt the bond between us flare with shared worry.

The Princess had recovered from her temper, and I felt her eyes assessing me as I turned back toward the door. "Bring another. Please." She now spoke in a much kinder tone that made me think perhaps she regretted her outburst. "I'll take it in the library."

My eyes darted to Aine's, and I knew she understood my meaning without words. She would find a way to be in the complement of servants in the library when I returned.

ROYALTY PAST, PRESENT, AND FUTURE

I brought a new tray from the kitchen a short while later and was surprised by the change in the Princess's mood. She was seated peacefully in a deep wooden chair, surrounded by many cushions and immersed in a thick tome that lay open in her hands. Aine stood off to her left, stiff and vigilant, every inch the personal guard of the Princess. It seemed that I was the only one who saw her as something other than what she projected. There were two young women sitting opposite on cushions, embroidering psalms onto linen altar cloths. All three looked up when I entered.

"I owe you a debt of gratitude, monsieur. It is not often that I behave like a shrew and nearly throw myself into the remains of my meal," she said, surprising me as well as all of the others in the room. Aine's eyes widened, and the ladies at her feet tucked their faces into their hands, smiling.

"Nay, Princess. Ye owe me nothing," I said, stammering. I placed the tray on a table near enough that she could reach when ready.

She looked down toward the ladies. "Leave us," she said. Neither commented, just picked up her work and moved silently away. The Princess did not speak until the door to the library had closed. "I don't know what came over me," she said. "It's de Nogaret. The man is a villain. He was so . . ." She stood and began to pace. "So pleased with himself and the bargain he made for my body and soul."

I found I could not stay silent in the face of her comment. "The man is foul, my Lady. Ye were a bit restrained, truly. I'm sure I'd have been worse if he were trading me off to the highest bidder."

Aine raised her eyebrows and darted a warning in my direction.

"You've had dealings with the man?" she asked.

I should not have spoken and now was caught in it. "Indirectly, my Lady, an' from the word of others who have cause to complain."

She stopped her pacing by a tall casement window that looked out over her father's land. As I took in her rigid stance and taut shoulders I wasn't thinking about much other than her eyes. Aine, however, was busy. I felt a slight vibration in the web of power surrounding the room and immediately set myself to joining her read as well as masking our use of the power.

There were many memories in this room, she was correct in that, but within the vibration I drew the essence that was the memory of the King. Almost at once I saw him there. My ears began to ring, and my vision slid back and forth between the present and the many instances of the King in this room in the past.

The Princess was absorbed in her thoughts, and we had a moment of freedom. Aine's song rang in my mind, soft and beautiful, the way it had so many times before, the way it hadn't since she'd left me. It felt good and right.

I drew the memory she identified most strongly with and expanded her sight of it with only the slightest effort.

The King stood before the shelves and reached behind a book with an old and cracked leather surface. A small metal box, ancient and tarnished, appeared in his palm. From inside the box came a bit of lead with two red silk strings attached. There was a shape embossed in it.

I edged closer to the shelf, peering with my other sight at the insignia that he saw. It was a man in a boat, fishing.

"Tell me about this land. Tell me about England and what I will have to face there." The words of the Princess jolted me from the vision of her father into a vision of her future. I jerked, surprised, as she stared at me. The

Princess Isabella on the royal throne of England. A golden crown low upon her brow. A child on her lap. And yet sadness was etched upon her brow.

"Ye will be Queen," I said. "Ye will have a son. He will be everything to ye."

Aine gasped. The Princess tipped her head and moved closer to peer up at me. "Are you a seer?" she asked softly. The question had such desperation to it that I could not find it in myself to lie.

"Aye, my Lady. Not in everything, but I see some things." My words were a whisper.

"No," said Aine.

The Princess turned, and with a nod of her head, Aine was dismissed from the room. As Aine reluctantly moved past me, the swirl of her worry worked its way around my mind. There was nothing I could do now, however, for the Princess knew and was determined to find out more.

TRUTH AND PROMISES

"Why are you here?" the Princess asked the moment we were alone in the library.

Her gaze was direct, and I was compelled to answer truthfully, though I questioned the wiseness of doing so.

"My Lady, I am seeking my brother. He was abducted from my homeland near on a full moon past." I walked toward the shelves, drawn to the spot I had seen in the vision.

"You seek him here? Why?" she asked, watching my movements as if she were a hawk ready to swoop.

I hesitated. "I have reason to believe he was taken by agents o' yer father."

She stared at me as if to decide if I had taken leave of my senses or was actually telling her the truth. "Is there somewhere that requires you now? This tale is one I think that will take some time in the telling."

I hesitated. Why was I here, telling her things that could get not only myself, but also many of the people I knew killed? "Perhaps I misspoke. I should be going, my Lady." I turned from the shelves, intent on the door.

"No, wait. You must tell me more. I need to know. . . ." She seemed unsure of herself at that moment, sad somehow, and my heart twisted just a bit. I did not know why I should relate to someone like her or care. But perhaps she was just as misused as we.

"If I can tell it, my Lady, I will. What is it that ye need to know?" I had somehow come to stand in front of her and in that moment she was not royalty, not a Lady, not a Queen to be. She was just a lass, and her eyes shimmered with tears unshed.

"Will I love him?" Her question came out as a soft entreaty.

I stared deep into her eyes and made the decision. Then, for the first time I called upon the power and drew a vision to me as I had never done before. The library faded, and I found myself a witness in the private suite of the future King of England. The Princess was Queen.

"*Why are you only happy when another is at your side?*" she asked.

"*Don't ask what you do not want to hear, Isabella. We are husband and wife, you and I. We do not dislike each other. I do not mistreat you.*"

"*But you do not love me,*" she whispered. The future King walked from their bedchamber without a backward glance.

I came back to the library with a lurch, to the golden amber of her pleading eyes, and God help me I could not tell her the truth of what I'd seen. Her hope was too strong.

Instead, I found myself leaning toward her, her breath soft on my lips and my hands barely touching her shoulders. And in the next moment I found myself kissing the Princess, daughter of the King of France, the future Queen of England. I was the first to pull away, shocked by what I'd done. Isabella appeared dazed. Her hand rose gently to her lips, her eyes lit with the glow of the sun.

"I'm sorry. I'd better go," I said, and quickly made my way to the door.

"Wait," she said.

My hand rested weakly on the latch.

"Who are you?" she asked.

I turned back only a moment. "I am no one, my Lady. Just the son o' a fisherman." I opened the door and was through it before she could speak another word.

Aine waited in the shadows and fell into step beside me as I walked. "What did ye tell her?" she hissed.

"I sought her help in finding Torquil," I said, avoiding all other mention of what had happened.

"Have ye taken leave o' yer senses?" she demanded. "She will have yer head for witchcraft. How could ye have spoken o' a vision to the Princess?"

"Aine, I didn't do it on purpose," I said, annoyed. "It came to me, an' I was no' o' a right mind to brush it off." I waved my hand in a dismissive manner. "She doesn't even know who I am. What does it matter?"

I could feel Aine stewing beside me. "No good will come o' this. Mark my words."

ROYAL INTEREST

Cornelius carved a bit of wild peahen, then speared it with his knife. "There is talk among the kitchen staff that the Princess is seeking a worker who delivered food to her on the eve o' this day past." He grinned. " 'Tis said she is quite ardent in her search." He raised his eyebrows. "Is there anyone here who would answer to that description?"

I ducked away from his questioning gaze, seeking a place of peace to think about the golden eyes that haunted my morning. Aine had arrived early, and I had never seen a sourer disposition on her. I avoided her company but could not escape her gaze.

"Tormod, I thought that we agreed that ye would stay in the suite," said the Templar. "The last thing we need right now is the Princess seeking ye out."

"I needed to warn Aine that Gaylen was here," I said. "There was no other way, truly."

The Templar made a noise low in his throat. I knew it well for disbelief and a bit of annoyance.

Aine sat on the dais, scowling at me. I took a seat on the bench near the rear wall and idly fished out a book on ancient tales that the Templar had been reading, but my mind refused to focus on the words before me.

"Aine, have ye had any progress in the library?" the Templar asked.

I had nearly forgotten. "We were able to expand the vision last night, together. The object the King holds is a circular bit o' lead with silk strings attached," I said. "On it is the image o' a boat with a man fishing from it."

The Templar looked up with surprise. "An impression o' the ring o' the fisherman, the Holy Father's ring?"

"Why would the King have something like that?" Aine asked.

"More to the point, why would he keep it hidden?" Alexander replied. I knew the far-off expression he wore — his mind was working furiously for an answer. "Were there any markings around the edge?"

"We saw only the vision o' the memory. The King did not look at what he held very closely," I replied.

"Aine, d'ye know the Princess's schedule today? Is there any way ye can get back into the library in safety?"

Aine fidgeted. "I can try, but the Princess has broken from her routine today. She spent longer than usual abed and took a stroll near the kitchens after she broke her fast." Aine's gaze flickered toward me, and I felt the heat rise in my face.

The Templar rose swiftly and moved with purpose toward the door. "I must speak to Fabienne about the King's feast this evening. Cornelius, will ye accompany me?" he asked.

"Of course, Alexander. I have a new pouch o' saffron she requested."

"We will be out for a short while." The Templar turned to me pointedly. " 'Tis important that ye are no' seen, Tormod. Do we understand one another?"

His tone stung. I nodded, determined to show him that I was listening and responsible.

Once the Templar and Cornelius left, there was a quiet in the suite that was less than comfortable. Aine sat by the window, staring out without speaking. Her shielding was strong and high — I could get nothing of what she was feeling or thinking.

"She asked me to give ye this." I scarcely heard the words she spoke and so was surprised when she rose abruptly and dropped a small, folded bit of parchment into my lap.

"Who?" I asked.

Her eyes flashed, and I blinked at the venom revealed there. "The Princess," she hissed.

"What does it say?" I asked, flipping it open.

"How would I know that, Tormod? I canno' read, as ye are so fond o' announcing to the world." There was anger as well as hurt in her tone, and I was ashamed of myself.

"I'm sorry. When this is a' last put to rest, I will teach ye if I can." I read the note, and when I looked up at her I was surprised to see the film of tears in her eyes. She quickly turned away, and her voice was thick when she spoke.

"What does it say?"

I felt as though a pile of sand was lodged within my throat. "She wants to meet me. She says 'tis about my brother."

Nervousness flared between us as Aine unconsciously lowered her shields. "Where? When?"

A RENDEZVOUS
WITH A PRINCESS

We had to wait until lauds had finished, and the Princess had returned from the Queen's chapel with the rest of her ladies-in-waiting. Aine stood beyond the library door, watching for trouble as I slipped inside. I had little reason to be in this room alone, but the servants of the Princess adored her. Blind eyes were turned in my direction on the strength of her request.

The library was empty, and I moved quickly toward the shelves. The cracked spine of the old book crumbled a bit beneath my fingers as I edged it aside. The dust behind was thick. I felt it on my tongue and in my nose as I slid my fingers into the darkened space. The metal box was hard and gritty. And for a reason I could not fathom, a prickle of cold ran along my neck.

I slid the book back in place just as a door I had not known to be there swung open to my left. The space behind it was dark, and as she emerged it was as if light came into the room. "Princess," I said, dipping low in a bow.

"You know who I am, but I do not have that advantage, monsieur." She took my hand and drew me up from the bow. For an awkward moment I held her fingers, then dropped them as if they burned. She turned and moved toward the chair I knew her to be fond of reading in. Her dress was of the finest silk in a shade of green that made the white of her skin and the gold of her eyes glow. I found it difficult to look away but forced myself to do it. This was truly an uncomfortable situation to be in.

"Your name. Would you never have me know it?" she said.

I battled with myself and what I knew to be safe, but beneath her gaze I could do nothing but speak the truth. "I am Tormod MacLeod, my Lady. Just a fisherman's son from a land far from yer shores."

"Tormod," she repeated. "It is an interesting name. In my language would it have a different translation?" I was captivated by the way my name sounded coming from her lips.

"Thomas, I believe, my Lady," I replied.

She nodded. "I prefer your language, monsieur, and the way you speak it. Yesterday you spoke of something." She hesitated. "Something you saw of my life in the time to come."

My heart raced, but I said nothing. "If I asked you to tell me more, would you?" she said softly.

"I don't believe that I would, my Lady," I said. "In part for the reason that I canno' command the future to speak its knowledge to me, but also because 'tis, in my experience, no bargain to know what is to come."

"And if I commanded it of you?" she asked, her golden gaze direct and compelling.

I returned the look with a smile. "I would beg to decline, my Lady."

"If I could do a favor for you," she said, "would you in return try once again for me?"

My heart nearly seized in my chest. "What favor?" I asked, breathless, knowing that it was for this I had come.

"Your brother. Give me his name and I will find out if he is being held here or anywhere near."

I could not speak for the hope that suddenly soared within my chest. "And if he were, is there anything you could do to gain his freedom?"

She broke the lock of our gazes and looked off toward the door to the hall. "I cannot guarantee anything, but I will swear to you that I will try."

I moved toward the chair that had swallowed her up and made her look small and innocent and had to remind myself that appearances could be deceiving. I did not know this lass and I had very little reason to put my trust in her. "Princess, 'tis very dangerous for my name to be known here a' court," I said. "Can ye be discreet in yer inquiry?" I was beside her then, and my hand had somehow come to be on the arm of her chair.

"Tormod, what would my father have you arrested for? Why was your brother taken?" I was unsure what to say. "Does it have something to do with this ability you have?"

I could not answer directly. Too much was at stake. She was the daughter of my enemy and a powerful entity on her own. "I would be burned as a witch if you spoke the slightest word," I warned.

Her soft hand closed over mine, and I felt the strength within her. "I would be careful for you. Have we a bargain?"

I turned my hand over and she clasped it, her fingers a soft caress in my own. "God help me, we do," I said.

DISCOVERY AND DECEPTION

The Princess slipped behind the secret door and disappeared from sight just as Aine let herself into the room from the corridor. "Someone is coming," she said, rushing to my side. "Pick up the tray an' act as if ye were returning to the kitchen." She quickly moved to the chair of the Princess and began tidying the cushions. As her hand skimmed the arm of the chair, her body jerked and her eyes grew wide. I felt her song hang silent in the air.

Aine's mouth fell open and a swirl of hurt rushed through her. I saw the images she did in that moment, fingers entwined, standing closely together, and then as

Aine turned to the shelves the memory echo of the kiss we had shared hung in the air between us. She gasped and her cheeks flamed. Hurt, denial, and anger all crashed within her.

I heard the footsteps approaching. "Come. Quickly, here." I opened the secret door and pulled her, unresisting, into the darkness beside me. The odd passageway was close, and the dust we had displaced puffed up and slid inside my throat and nose. Aine was stiff beside me, trying her best not to have any part of my body touch hers. I normally would have taken her hand in a situation like this, but knowing what she had seen take place between the Princess and myself, I kept my arms leaden and by my sides.

I was unsure where the passage led, but still might have drawn Aine along, had I not known her temper as I did. With the Princess more than likely near the exit, I thought it a better idea to stay right where we were. Beyond the door, I heard movement in the library, the slip of feet on the stones of the floor and the click of the latch as the door closed.

"Have you secured the location of the Templar records? We need to know where all of the Order's gold and jewels are hidden."

I pressed my ear to the door. The voice was

de Nogaret's. "The Abbot is strong in his faith, my Lord Chief Counselor. He has as yet held out many of the secrets you asked us to retrieve."

"No man can endure the torture of the King's dungeons. Use all of the instruments at your disposal. I want a complete list. Every holding. Every land. Every coin. To the last," he said. "Above all, I want the Vessels of Holiness. The Abbot knows their location. My buyer is most insistent that they be delivered to him before the King will have the support that he requires. Get that information at all cost."

"Yes, my Lord Chief Counselor." The door opened and closed once more and Aine and I stood as still as stone waiting for sound from beyond. Footsteps murmured on the stones close to the shelves. Listening hard, I heard the scrape of volumes as they were drawn from the shelves. The breath in my chest felt as if to seize.

Then from beyond the door came the sound of another. "Come, Beatrice. I long for a good tale and the peace of my chair." The creak of the door sounded as the Princess and her ladies trooped inside.

"What business have you here, de Nogaret?" Her derision was plain and, I thought, dangerous.

"Good day, Princess," he said pleasantly. "Just looking for a book for your father. It was such a relief to hear from your betrothed, wouldn't you say? Just think, by spring you will be wedded in bliss . . . in a foreign land." The last bit he said in a flat and unyielding manner.

No response came from the Princess, just the sound of the door latching shut behind him.

"Follow me," I whispered to Aine. The walkway was tight and twisting and led away deep into the heart of the castle, its passage as black as night and as cold as a crypt. Aine was silent, but I felt the quick warm brush of her breath on my neck and the occasional hand to my shoulder, when I moved faster or slower than she anticipated.

My mind was a blur. We had just heard de Nogaret authorize the torture of the Abbot. If Torquil was here, what had he already been through? I expected Aine to read my anxiousness and somehow make it better, but she was as if a ghost to me. She spoke not at all and from the moment we had entered the passage her shields had become impregnable. I didn't know what to say to her. Should I try to explain what had happened? Should I tell her what I had seen of the Princess's future or of the conversation we had?

Moments stretched and I was no closer to answers when the corridor came to an abrupt halt. We stopped and listened, but beyond where we stood there was no noise at all. I took a breath and held it as I pressed against the wall before me. Slowly, it eased forward and I crept beyond with Aine a sliver of shadow at my back.

BLESSED ART THOU

The room was dark but for the flicker of two small candles beside the statue of the Lady Mother. It was a high-vaulted room with a small wooden altar carved lovingly with many kinds of bird and beast. Fine tapestries hung to the right and left of us, filling the walls with the muted colors of the forest. Crisp white linens covered the altar and the base of the statue, and the dark smelled of recently burning herbs.

The Queen's chapel. Of all the spaces in the castle, this one provided me with a sense of peace and goodness that I had not found anywhere else. Aine wandered from my side and stood transfixed, staring up at the statue. "Tormod," she whispered suddenly, gripping the altar's edge. "Does this remind ye o' anything?"

I approached slowly, a strange prickle of awareness sliding over my skin and making me shiver. "She looks like the carving," she said softly. The air seemed to leave my body in a rush. I had no idea how it was so, but Aine, who had only seen the ancient relic through the memory of my visions, was right. And her assessment brought a strange wonder and excitement to my entire being. I had been so close to it that I had never guessed, never truly seen, but the clues had been there all along.

The visions had shown me a young man, a carver, who had made a likeness of his mother and gifted her with it. Who more than a carpenter's son, would have the artistry and the capability to carve such a likeness? The carver had been our Lord Jesus and the carving made in the likeness of Our Lady.

I could see in my mind the real woman, who had come to me sometimes through the visions. Her hair had been a deep and vibrant chestnut that curled in waves about her face. Her eyes had been a brilliant brown, like the bark of a rowan tree, and in them I had seen warmth, compassion, and love.

I stared with rapt attention at the statue before me. The likeness between the woman, the original carving, and this full-size statue was astounding. I wondered how many inspired and sacred images of Our Lady there were in the world. Did each have some essence of the woman's spirit inside? I dropped to my knees, and Aine joined me there.

Our Lady full of grace . . . I made no excuse or apology to Aine for my sudden devotion. She, too, was moved to add her voice to my prayers. In my head I called to Her. *My Lady, Mother o' the Lord, what would Ye ask o' Yer servant?*

I could sense nothing from the wooden statue before me, but along the bond between the carving and myself, I felt a sudden flare of heat. The need to hold it once more was like a hunger that came on quickly and churned within every inch of my body. At once the chapel faded and I found myself in the darkened space below the ancient broch that Aine and I had stumbled upon in Scotland. The hard surface of the polished table was beneath my knees and before me lay the odd, deadened space that I remembered feeling in that place before.

The vision faded as quickly as it had come, leaving me with an answer of sorts, but one I was not at all certain about. I stood and held out my hand to Aine. And with a gaze filled with wonder, she took my fingers in her own and rose.

"Ye saw it as well?" I asked in a whisper.

"Aye," she replied. "Ye must bring the pieces there."

"But how will I get the carving back from Gaylen?" I asked.

"I don't know, but perhaps the Lady will help." Her words were cryptic, and I wondered if she meant the carving or the Princess. She dropped my hand then and moved in the dark toward the door, once again as far from me as she had been in the corridor between the walls.

ROYAL INTERCESSION

Fabienne was in Cornelius's suite when we returned, flanked by the Templar and the seamstress. Lisette sat on a low stool not far away, as silent and watchful as ever. The Templar looked up at me when we entered, and the knowledge that a very long and painful discussion on obedience would be happening between us very soon, haunted me.

"Aine, yer services to the Princess are no longer required," he said abruptly.

"But —" she said on a gasp, and her eyes flew to mine. The question hung between us. How would the Princess make contact if Aine was not there anymore?

He continued. "A wardrobe will be made for ye, an' yer hair addressed. Fabienne has a wig that will make it appear long. Ye will be presented to the King tonight, so come an' be measured. There is much to be done."

As the Templar passed by me, he said softly, "An' ye will stay in our suite with a guard set a' the door, so that ye are no' tempted to wander." I felt as though he had landed a blow to my stomach. There was so much I needed to tell him, but I could not address any of it with Fabienne, Lisette, and a seamstress in the suite. The Templar was acting as if I were the enemy. I was confused. I sat on the bench that ran along the far wall, the cold of the stones at my back nothing compared to the chill that had filled my body.

Aine stood before the seamstress with a blank expression. She had not turned my way, nor spoken since our exchange in the Queen's chapel. Her shields were high and I could not sense her emotion, but it was easy to guess that she was still thinking about my dealings with the Princess.

Though I should have, by rights, been thinking of ways to get the carving back from Gaylen, my mind continued to drift back to those moments as well. The kiss we had shared was an oddity I was having trouble reconciling. The Princess had been sad, I reasoned, and I had wanted to give her comfort. She smelled nice and was soft against me, and I could not help but compare her kiss to Aine's.

I watched her now, beneath lowered lids. The kiss of the Princess had been like the flame of a candle, I decided, where Aine's kisses had been like wildfire. Though Aine could not know it, I preferred to be burned.

Dinner with the King was a monumental occasion at court, though if asked, I knew that none of our party saw it as a boon. For the whole of the afternoon, I waited to get the Templar alone to tell him what had happened, but he had left Cornelius's suite soon after we arrived and did not return at all. I waited in frustration, and paced the rooms, agitating both Bran and Aine.

In the end, Cornelius, tired of listening to the barking and bickering, escorted me back to our rooms where a footman of the guard was now stationed. I had no idea what the Templar had told the man or how he had been commissioned, but I had the firm knowledge that his duty was interpreted in one way: I was not to be allowed to leave. I was on edge and annoyed. I was not a bairn to be sent to my pallet.

The Templar had already been here, I noticed. His clothes of the day lay in a pile on the basket of laundry, waiting to be fetched by the palace servants, and the fine linens and silks for court dinners were missing from the wardrobe. I flopped into a chair by the hearth, brooding, where I remained for several interminable marks of the candle.

"Stand aside," said a voice I recognized from the corridor. My heart leapt and I hurried toward the door.

"But, mademoiselle —" the guard began.

"You will address me as milady or my Princess," she commanded loftily. "Now remove yourself from this door or you will be turned out for the winter." She spoke with an authority I doubted any would question.

"*Oui*, milady Princess," he replied quickly. The clink of a sword accompanied the shuffle of booted feet. I dropped to a bow as the door opened, feeling as skittish as a colt ready to run. What was she doing here? How had she tracked me down in a castle as large and filled as this?

The door swung shut with a creak, and I rose, uncertain what I would see when I did. The Princess was alone. "Ye're resourceful, my Lady Princess," I said, wondering how it was that I was speaking to her so comfortably.

What might have passed as a smile flitted across her face, but was replaced just as quickly by tightly pressed lips. "You disappeared, as did my manservant," she said softly. "I had to find you."

I tipped my head, questioning, and she came to me quickly and seized my hands. My pulse leapt with alarm. "Tormod, he is here. God help him. Your brother is in the lower dungeons and has been there for some time."

Suddenly, the visions I had come to fear more than any other rose up and filled my world with an agony so deep that I dropped to the floor of the suite and cried out. The Princess was before me, but I could no longer see her.

The smell was sharp and all around me: dirt, blood, sweat, and urine. I gagged and the movement stretched the cracked and weeping skin of my back. I screamed deep in my mind as the pain of burns and whip marks stripped all thought from my head.

Ground, damn ye! Tormod, distance yerself! The Templar was in my mind, and yet I could not pull myself from my brother. I saw him as I felt him, stripped and huddled in the blackness. His fingers and toes were raw where the rats had bitten. His back was afire, the skin broken and weeping. I reached for his mind to give whatever help I might, but was immediately repelled.

No. The shout in my head was tortured and rasping. *Get far from here. Now, Tormod!* And with what I could feel was the last of his strength, he drew the power beneath the castle into his mind and forced me out.

"By God, no. I'll not leave ye here." I sat slowly, remembering at last that the Princess was still here, her hands still entwined with mine, her eyes filled with worry. I squeezed her fingers and released them. "I have to get down there. I've got to get him out."

"I will help you, I swear it." Her expression was earnest and I nodded.

"And I will need it." I stood. "But ye must go now. How can I reach ye again?" I had to get her out of here. The Templar would not be long away.

"The boy who serves in the kitchens. Send your messages through him, and I will do the same." She gathered up her skirts and moved to the door.

"My Lady Princess?" I asked. She paused and stared at me. "Thank ye."

She nodded and was gone.

THE SUPPORT OF FRIENDS

"He is here. And I will wait no more for the politics an' the help that would come from all yer meetings an' plans," I said when the Templar had barely breached the door.

"Rash actions bring severe consequences, Tormod. I know that ye're worried an' frustrated."

"This is my brother," I snapped. "He has been beaten, burned, an' bitten by rats. All in my name. I canno' bear it." I grasped my head in my hands. "I can still hear it. I can feel it, Alexander."

"Ye must push it aside, Tormod. Ye are not alone in this. We will work together. But ye must control yerself!"

My mind was already far away, thinking of a way that the Princess could get me into the dungeon. I didn't care if I had to take Torquil's place. I would go to him tonight.

"Don't make me lock ye in here," he said. I was not surprised that he knew my thoughts. He always did.

I met his eye squarely. "Then that is what ye must attempt, Alexander, for I will not be stopped in this."

He sighed and sat down in the deep chair beside me. "Together, Tormod. We go in together as brothers as we have been from the beginning." He offered me his hand and I took it.

"We have the Princess with us as well," I said as the door to the suite opened.

"An' ye have me," said Aine.

"An' me," said Cornelius.

"We will find a way," Alexander said.

DARKNESS AND DUNGEONS

I followed the Princess with a screen of blankness surrounding me. Aine and the Templar Alexander joined my efforts, gently drawing power from beneath the castle, each working to offset the other, both hiding me and all trace of their meddling as I focused only on myself and what needed to be done. It was a difficult task for me, for I was shielding not only the physical appearance of my body, but fear for my brother and my anger at his treatment.

"This is quite irregular, my Princess. The dungeons are no place for you." The guard feared for her safety and so to whisper that he didn't feel that way would not work. I had to dig deeper and come up with a notion he would believe. *You will protect me. I am unafraid.* His hand closed more tightly on the hilt of his dagger and he stood taller and straighter.

The stairs to the dungeon were brightly lit, and scores of the King's guard stood at attention as we passed. I heard the murmur of "milady" and "Lady

Princess" said in shocked whispers, and it took everything I had to keep the whisper flowing.

"Lady Princess, the lower dungeons are foul pits. Will you not change your mind and leave the healer to see to those vermin?" The man rubbed his ears vigorously. My whispered suggestion that he allow the Princess below made him itch.

"The healers are busy seeing to the retinue of the Holy Father. All men are God's children, monsieur, even if they are deep in our dungeons doing penance for their mistakes. It is my duty as Princess to show what pity I can." Her speech was delivered with heartfelt sincerity. Even without the whisper the man would be hard pressed to deny her golden gaze. "We will begin at the bottom and work our way up. I will take no chances, and you will protect me." She shifted the grain sack filled with bandages, herbals, poultices, and simples.

The air changed as we descended the old and broken stairs that led to the deepest levels of the dungeons. Cold dampness warred with the rotted smell of bodies, sickness, and human waste. The remainder of my dinner lodged itself in the top of my throat, and I fought the waves of nausea that pummeled me at the scent. The Princess had blanched a sickly shade of white, but to her credit she continued the descent.

The dim light of only a few torches broke the darkness below. The cells were cast in almost total blackness and as we came on the first, the soldier warned the Princess back. "Hold, milady." He moved ahead toward the iron grate and thrust his torch into the first of the cells. "On your feet! You have a visit from the Royal Princess." The old man in the cell was covered in filth, and the stench of him watered my eyes. His hair had grown so long that it hung in filthy ropes over his chest and down to his waist. An odd chittering sound came from his mouth, and he huddled close on himself, rocking back and forth.

"Your pity is wasted on that one, Princess," the guard said. "He's already got a foot in the other world and his mind is gone."

She stood at the grate holding the bars. The cell was barely large enough to hold him lying flat, and there was no way the low ceiling could allow him to stand at his full height. "Leave him this bread. And double the water."

The soldier grimaced but answered, "As you wish, my Princess," and we moved along. Each cell was as bad as the first, and the Princess was moved to enter several. None of the prisoners tried to harm her — most were so badly starved that they could barely lift their heads. To these she called for a bucket of water and ladle to administer the drink herself. She seemed to care naught for the muck that muddied her dress nor the rank filthiness of the men to whom she ministered. As for myself, I was desperate for her to advance. I could feel Torquil ahead and though I would have moved past her and on to him alone, I didn't want to raise alarm.

Sweat rolled down my neck as I steadily pulled the power to continue. I was light-headed, and my knees shivered with the effort. Torquil was badly wounded. I could feel his pain and to help him endure was drawing it into myself. The burns were the worst. My feet felt as if they were twice their size and pulsed with agony.

He was in the fourth cell that we came to and I nearly sobbed at the sight of him. Torquil was barely alive. His face was grotesquely broken and swollen as he lay in the mud where he had fallen. His clothes were stuck to the open and seeping lash marks on his back, and his breeks were dark where he had wet himself beneath the torture. The skin on his legs was black, and his feet were red and covered with blisters.

"Dear Lord, this man needs help," said the Princess. "Let me in."

"I beg your pardon, milady, but this one is overseen by the Councillor de Nogaret. It is by his order that none are to go near." The man was nervous, afraid to get between the Princess and de Nogaret.

"Last I knew I outranked the King's Keeper of the Seal, monsieur. Open the door. Now." The Princess stood tall and imperious, every inch a royal personage.

The door to the cell was quickly opened, and I circled her as she entered and dropped to his side, holding back the tears that, if allowed, would banish my shielding. I sent a tentative probe into his mind. *Torquil. Can ye hear me?*

His eyes fluttered but did not rise and his voice did not greet mine, even mind to mind. I looked to the Princess and motioned that she drop the bag and kneel to cover me. Then quickly I fished inside for the vial that the Templar had Fabienne purchase in the markets. The black liquid had no smell, but of its properties I had been taught. Just a drop, beneath the tongue. I unstoppered the vial and dipped my finger inside, then quickly I opened his mouth and applied it. The Princess took clean linens from her bag and soaked them in water from her flask. Carefully, she stripped the tunic from his back and gently cleaned the welts and applied salve. The legs were beyond her ability and so she was only able to apply ointment to his feet.

All the while the Princess worked on Torquil from the outside the Templar, Aine, and I worked on him from the inside. Power flowed in an unending stream through the floor of the dungeon into my body and out through my fingertips. There I directed it with my mind to the areas most damaged, focusing most on the skin and muscle of his legs.

"I fear this is for naught, Princess. This one is beyond help and I for one do not want to face the Lord Councillor if he should expire while we are about." I had stopped the whisper of the guard to help Torquil and the suggestion was wearing off. "I think you have done enough good for one day." He was lifting her bag and drawing her up from the ground.

She looked at me and I nodded. Together we quit the cell without a word.

PRAYERS AND GOOD-BYES

The wait during the rest of the night was unbearable. Much of it was spent on my knees, praying to the Lord that our plan would come off as hoped. There were so many things that could go wrong, the slightest unforeseen circumstance.

Aine knelt at my side, uncharacteristically quiet. At times, she reached over and laid a hand on my arm and I was calmed. We hadn't spoken of anything and, in truth,

I wanted nothing but to be left alone with the thoughts of my brother. Gaston arrived long after dark with a message from the Princess. I was to meet her in the library within a candle mark. The time to repay her had come.

As I slipped from the suite, I felt Aine's eyes on me.

The library was dark when I arrived. I couldn't get the images of Torquil out of my mind, and my guts churned once more. The soft voice of the Princess broke the stillness in the room. "I've never seen anything like that before in my life."

I moved toward the sound and found her curled up in a chair by the blackened hearth. I knelt before her. "An' I pray ye never will again, my Lady," I said softly.

"He was your brother," she said.

"He *is* my brother, Princess. He still lives." I said it forcefully. I needed to hang on to the belief with all my heart and soul. She nodded.

"I have paid that guard to come to me if anything should happen to the prisoner," she said, her words hollow.

I lifted a hand and cupped her face. "Then ye should be in yer rooms, for we both know that message will come tonight." She rested her head against me a moment. "Gaston will sleep outside yer chambers in the hall. Send word when ye hear."

"But they will not release him until morning no matter what," she said. It was frigid outside, and it would be a better thing if that were true.

"But if 'tis earlier, I need to know. Please, tell me ye will send word. No matter what time o' night or morning," I said.

"Of course. Tormod . . ." She hesitated and I brushed her cheek with my fingertips. "I don't want to know. I've decided. I don't want to know what is to come of my life. Whatever it is will be more than the poor, tortured souls that I saw today. And perhaps, when I am Queen, I can put an end to this kind of suffering."

I drew her face up so that she was forced to meet my eyes. "Ye will make a wonderful Queen." I sighed deeply. "The future is not something that is etched in stone. What I see might happen, but it also may never, an' so 'tis pointless to seek what is to come."

She nodded. "Will you leave here? Will I ever see you again?" There were many things in her eyes, questions that I had no power to answer.

"I am to be a Knight Templar. I return to my home as soon as I finish the things I have come here for." She lifted her face from my hand. "And ye will become a

Queen," I said. "I will forever be grateful for all that ye have done today."

"It is I who am grateful. What you have shown me today is that I have lived a sheltered and pampered life. From this night on, I will not be content to sit, read, and embroider. And those who would use the King's power to further their ambitions will be brought to justice." She was far away already, thinking beyond this day and this room.

"I must be getting back. Ye'll send word?" I asked again.

She nodded and stood before me. I dipped to my knee and kissed her fingers. "Thank ye, my Lady Princess." She was a bit saddened. I could feel it projecting from her, but our places had been established, she as future Queen, and me as a Knight Templar. No more was written.

"Good-bye, Tormod."

THE DEATH PITS

The Templar was on his way into the village to procure the wagon, blankets, and healer's ointments that Fabienne had arranged. She, Lisette, and Gaston had quit the palace at daybreak, heading for their estates up north, where we were to meet them. I stood among the trees, ankle deep in fresh snow that had fallen since we arrived. Gaston had sent word from the Princess midway through the night.

I trembled in the cold, terrified that something had not gone according to plan. Staring at the great pit outside the rear of the castle, the gruesome specter of what I was about to see, made me want to vomit.

My blood ran cold when I heard the clink of the rusted grate as it slid into place, and I held my breath as the first was shoved out the door and into the pit. It was the ragged old man from the first cell. His body was stiff and when he hit the frozen ground his head twisted at an impossible angle, the eyes still wide in the last moments of his death. I gasped and moved out from the cover of the trees, praying that no one would notice, though against the white of the landscape I was far from hidden.

The door remained open, and two men emerged, complaining about the duty they had been assigned to. "This one's a mess, he is. Don't get it on me."

"Shut up and lift him beneath the arms. He's awkward as Hades."

"His back's covered in blood. It's not like they will let me go back for a fresh sark. Let's just kick him out from here." My heart began to beat furiously and I took several crouched steps, ready to run if it came to it.

"Just lift the bastard. I'd like to get on and break my fast," the first grumbled. And with that, the body of my brother was tossed from the platform to land on top of the heap. From what I could see it was a clean throw, though he landed facedown in the snow. The gate closed, signaling that no others had died in the night, and I hurried to where they'd thrown Torquil.

I bolted over the hilly rise directly into the pit, my feet slipping in the snow, slowed by the many odd shapes that were beneath it. Bodies were frozen sólid. Some large, some small, some whose eyes seemed to follow me as I climbed my way to the hill where two freshly dead had joined them. I found the old man first and did not stop, though I had the mad desire to straighten his neck. And then I found Torquil.

It was one thing to know that I had given him a dose of poison that would stop his heart, another altogether to see him facedown and dead, one body in a pile of many. I whipped him over onto his back and quickly checked to see that he had not been further molested. The Princess had said that de Nogaret was furious. He had obviously not gotten the information he would have liked from Torquil. It would take nothing for a man such as he to do further damage to a dead man just to make himself feel better.

Torquil looked the same as he had when I last saw him, though his face was an unearthly shade of white, and he did not appear to be breathing. Quickly, I drew the vial from my sporran, an antidote to the poison that had set him into the deep sleep they had mistaken for death. "Come on, Torquil," I coaxed, prying his mouth open and forcing the liquid into his throat. There was no reflex that would make him swallow the drug, but having it inside his throat and in contact with the soft tissues there was supposed to be enough to make it absorb into his body.

Several moments crawled by and there was no reaction to the liquid. My heart began to pound forcefully. "Come on, brother, ye will live." I spoke around my chattering teeth, my mind frantic with the possibility that I had been too late.

Nothing. One heartbeat. Two. My mind was racing. "Please. Please. Please." I was holding tight to his tunic, begging. "Lady, help me!" I called to the Holy Mother, whose echo of power lived on in the carving. I knew that it was somewhere within the walls of the castle. What I didn't know was that it was closer than I thought.

AN UNWELCOME VISITATION

"Once again ye're calling to an entity that will not help ye in any way."

I turned to Gaylen, sick with dread. "Give me the carving. I have to help him. He has nothing to do with this!" Every moment that passed by was a moment more that Torquil was under the extreme sedation. He had to be brought out of it soon.

"He involved himself. A pity," said Gaylen. "And since ye've seen fit to remove him from the King's reach, I believe that ye should take yer rightful place in the dungeon from whence he has come."

"Please, I'll give ye whatever ye want. Tell ye whatever ye need. Use it to help him. Ye don't even have to give it to me. Have ye no compassion a' all?" I was so angry and desperate that I wanted to lunge for him. "What kind o' man sells his soul to see another gain a throne? He's my brother. Have ye never loved anyone?"

"I have known love, Tormod. All I do is in its name. Robert the Bruce will be King o' Scotland if I have to give over every dear mother, brother, and son to make it so."

I felt the heat of the carving and suddenly saw the memory as if his perfect shielding never existed. English forces had butchered his family while he was made to watch. *"Tell your people that this is what will come of resistance,"* the English sergeant had said as he wiped the blood of Gaylen's brother on the sleeve of his tunic.

I pulled back, unsure why the carving was showing this to me. Gaylen had stolen the carving. He had given my brother up to this torture. How was I supposed to feel sympathy for him?

"I hold no illusions. I will burn in the fires o' hell for all I've done in the name o' vengeance, but I will take as many o' them as I can with me as I go."

"I am no' yer enemy, nor is my family."

"Touching, Tormod, but I care no' for any man. My oath is vengeance, and I will have it." He drew his sword from the sheath.

"Ye canno' barter the Holy Vessel in the wars o' men," I said.

"There ye are wrong. Its price is measured in gold an' the backing o' the King and Church. 'Tis a currency, as was yer brother, an' now ye." His sword danced close and I was forced to step away from Torquil to avoid the cut.

"I do no' have to deliver ye fully whole, Tormod. They will make ye burn an' bleed even if I cut the ears from yer head an' the arms from yer body." He took a step that brought him between Torquil and me. My heart beat fiercely just then for I saw a halting breath lift my brother's once-still chest.

"Why d'ye hate the Templars?" I asked.

He seemed taken aback by the question but answered without hesitation. "They are as easily bribed as any."

I felt a familiar heat wash through me. "Why do they want a list o' the holdings o' the Order from the Abbot?" I demanded, taking advantage of his confusion and advancing on him to push him away from Torquil.

He seemed surprised by the sudden flare of heat from the carving. I was not. I felt the bond I shared with it pulsing more strongly than ever before. I knew that it was in the pouch by his side, just as I knew suddenly that while it was on his body he would be forced to truthfully answer anything I asked of him. "The Templars will see their last days an' nothing ye will do can change the outcome, Tormod MacLeod." He seemed to recover his wits then and advanced on me once more. "Enough o' this. Yer brother is where he was destined to be, in the death pits, an' ye will come with me. De Nogaret will pay handsomely for the real Tormod MacLeod. He had little luck in getting the whereabouts o' the rest o' the Holy Relic from Torquil, but ye know where 'tis, an' ye will tell."

I edged back from the reach of his sword, stumbling over bodies as I reached for my dagger. It would be nothing against a sword unless I could get it away from him and move in close. Gaylen made a strong sweep toward me and I leapt aside, feeling the slice of my tunic. I moved wide to the left, circling him in a crouch. Alone and barely armed I was no match for him.

But suddenly I realized that I was not alone. I felt a rise in the earth's power coming from the carving. The familiar rush of its warmth brought the confidence that had, moments before, deserted me. Gaylen sensed the change at once and jammed his free hand into the pouch at his side. Startled, he quickly drew it out again.

"The carving's power is only to be used for good, Gaylen. 'Tis for healing an' truth. Any who have ever tried to subvert it for evil have paid. She is giving ye a warning."

With little effort I drew a near solid shield of heat and light around my brother and me. Gaylen's sword was no longer a threat. Fury pounded at my shields but I had little thought for him now. I crouched beside Torquil's body and felt for the beat of life at his neck.

The pulse was light and erratic, but there nonetheless, and I was glad of it. Torquil's skin, however, was so cold that it had a near bluish cast. Snow was pillowed beneath his head, and on his lashes ice had frozen.

"Stay with me, Torquil." I called the power with an authority I now knew to be mine. My fingertips tingled with the force of it as it flowed up from the land through the carving, into my mind, and out through my touch. At once the snow atop and beneath Torquil melted away. A body, frozen for the winter, lay beneath him and my stomach lurched in revolt. I closed my eyes and focused only on Torquil and began thrusting the sleeping draft out through his skin, following the paths of the sweat generated by the power's heat.

I could hear Gaylen cursing from beyond as he swung his sword to no end. The blade glanced off the shielding as if Torquil and I were encased in a wall of ice. Then, beneath my hands, Torquil began to stir, but the waking was not what I had anticipated. With awareness came the pain of his injuries, lashing our shared minds as one. It was all I could do to stay upright as I knelt over him. "Tormod," he cried softly. "End this now. I canno' bear it."

"Please, Torquil, just hold on. I can make it fade." I drew the pain into my body and immediately lurched as

I was assaulted with raw agony. I gasped and shook my head, trying to clear the haze of pain as I broke out in sweat. I could feel the shielding I held over us waver.

Drive the pain out of yer body an' into the earth. The Templar's voice was in my head and I felt his presence coming from somewhere down the road, beyond the trees. Aine's song suddenly filled me, and I could breathe once again. I could hear the conversation passing between them. *No, Aine, don't take it from him. He must disperse it. He is holding Torquil steady. If we dilute the hold it will harm the lad.* The pain came back at me full force and my arms and legs began to shake.

From beyond the shielding, I felt Gaylen gathering power, fighting to use the carving against me. He held it in his hands now, but I was controlling the flow and the heat pouring off it was burning him badly. "Ye will obey me! I am the holder." His voice cracked as he barked out the command.

With all of the pain coursing through me, I turned the power upon him. "If ye would use it," I said evenly, "ye will know the price."

To my surprise, I could see the vision that unfolded before Gaylen's eyes. A battle raged. Mounted Templar Knights, farmers, and lads, beat back a field of English soldiers. Bodies turned the grass red with blood. Gaylen fought, in the throes of a berserker fury, the bolt from a long bow lodged deeply in his chest.

I saw the carving fall from his fingers as shock rolled through him and he stumbled back. " 'Tis the devil," he whispered, staring at it with fear.

The worst of Torquil's pain was firmly grounded in the earth below my feet, and I found I could breath easily. "No, 'tis the light an' the truth," I said. "Ye have seen yer death this day. Is it not what ye imagined it to be?" A choking sound rattled from his lips, and his skin had grown pale, the blade in his hand all but forgotten. "Nothing ye have done will amount to glory, for ye will die impaled by an arrow on the day of —"

He turned and bolted down the slope. Though I did not have a date in mind for his death, he would never know. It was enough that he had seen it. It would take a man of complete faith to look upon the vision of his death without fear. Gaylen, I knew now, was no such man. The carving lay in the snow where he'd dropped it, black once more.

Torquil had slipped back into unconsciousness as I set to work on the worst of his injuries with renewed determination. And from the road came the sound of the wagon that carried friends.

RESCUE AND RECOVERY

Fabienne's estates were several leagues from the castle. I rode in the wagon next to Torquil, performing what healing I was able, with Aine sitting nearby settling his mind with her song. The carving was tucked securely in my sporran. The part of me that had been cut away was back and I was whole once more, but it did not ease my pain. We had arrived as the sun sank behind the hill, jostling up a road that led to the heart of her property.

The main house was grander than I would have imagined of someone who was not royalty. The enormity of what she risked to help the Templar and a group of strangers struck me as we entered. Her manservant opened wide the great wooden door and carefully the Templar and I carried Torquil inside. His body was slack in our arms, our grip and movement hampered by the care with which we had to move him.

The common room was warm, and I restlessly paced when I wasn't checking on Torquil's progress. He lay on his stomach on a cot as far from the fire as we could manage while still keeping him warm. The wounds on his feet and legs were horribly sensitive to heat. Every time he cringed and cried out in his sleep, my heart tore a little more. The welts on his back were a mass of yellow, black, blue, and red. It was too much to try and heal him all at one time, so I waited and paced until I could start again. I had steadied the worst of the trauma, but a fever lurked about, fighting my abilities. He had yet to gain consciousness, and I wanted to beat the walls with frustration.

"Tell me everything ye remember," said the Templar. "I know that yer memory is very good, Tormod. Ye told me that in the beginning."

So much had been going on. I struggled to recall the exact words that Gaylen had spoken. I stopped midstride. "I asked him why de Nogaret wanted the list o' Templar holdings an' he said, 'the Templars will see their last days an' nothing ye will do can change the outcome.'" The Templar was silent.

"We've got to get to the trainees. All o' this hinges on them in some way. I can feel it," I said. "Ye do as well. What is it that holds ye back?" The carving was glowing warm in my sporran. Aine and Fabienne both looked at him expectantly. "Let me go in as one o' them, Alexander. The Grand Master can arrange it. I can find out what they hide."

The Templar held my eyes, calculation strong in them. I did not expect him to agree with my idea, but nevertheless he said, "Do the next healing session on yer brother an' we will leave before vespers."

Aine looked up at me with fear in her eyes. As I moved to Torquil's side, she shifted with me. "Can we not just leave here?" she whispered. "We have what ye came for, both the carving an' yer brother. Let us leave these lands before something worse goes wrong."

I paused in my ministrations. "I canno' leave matters as they are, Aine. I am the chosen Protector o' the carving. She has been leading me on this journey from the beginning, an' I have to follow Her on to the end. There is still the matter o' the visions I've been granted. They are to work together as one, somehow, an' I believe the answer lies a' the preceptory with those three men." She leaned her head against my shoulder and for once comfort was not hers, but mine to give. "Here, help me now. There is still much healing to be done before I will be easy in leaving him."

DUTIES AND DECISIONS

Torquil was resting as comfortably as he could. There had been no fever for a long stretch of the early evening. Many of his body's wounds were on the mend, but I feared more the injury to his mind. I thought of Seamus and how he had been after a time with the King's torturer. Mayhap Aine was right, I should take him home so that my mam could tend him. How could I leave him this way, and go back for more trouble?

But if I did not go on to the preceptory, then all of this, all of the suffering and pain and struggle would account for nothing. I sat beside Torquil remembering each of the stages of the journey, calling to mind every bit of vision I could remember and trying to lay it out in some kind of order. There had been so many.

"Are ye ready?" The Templar stood before me holding a set of black apprentice robes. I reached for them with a shaking hand, the red of the cross calling to me as it had for the whole of my life. This was what I had waited for. And yet it was a farce. I was not in truth a

Templar's apprentice. I dropped the robe to my lap, saddened by the thought.

"Some apprenticeships are done in unconventional ways, Tormod. Ye are a Templar in all but the steps o' the rite, an' when all o' this is done, I will see to the omission."

I smiled wryly. If I didn't know better I would think that information was gleaned from a direct read of me.

"'Tis yer face, lad. There is so much expression there, yer mind is clear." He motioned to the robe. "Get ready. We should move quickly. It's a ride ahead o' us, an' I sent on a groom to ask for an audience with the Grand Master. We'd best not keep him waiting."

I rode beside the Templar, who at last wore his robes and armor openly. I took the black of apprentice with pride and honor. The land about us was thick with snow that had fallen through the afternoon and into the evening, but I had no eye for its beauty. Apprehension filled my every moment, between worry for Torquil and tension for the role I was about to play. I could see the outline of the wall and the rise of the dwellings beyond. "Will they know who ye are?"

"I haven't been here since I was a lad. This time of

night the chance that anyone might recognize me is less. I did not give my name, but the Order's code for emergency to the messenger." He stopped his horse and mine followed suit. "A rider approaches."

We sat our horses anxiously, watching the dark rider traverse the twisting road up from the preceptory. He rode quickly and directly to our place on the road, sidled up beside Alexander, and spoke. "The night has eyes."

"The Lord sees all," the Templar replied.

"We have been waiting for ye. The Grand Master is in the sacristy off the chapel. I will take you now." The man did not wait for an answer but turned his mount back down the road with us trailing.

The sacristy was a small room where the brothers kept the robes for prayer and the sacrament of the Lord. Beyond the cupboards built into the wall, there was only a small table and a single chair to fill the space. Several candles lit the room and in the chair sat the Grand Master, Jacques de Molay.

We had met once before, and at the time I had the poor luck to have a frightful vision of the man burning at the stake. It was not something either of us would ever forget. Alexander went down on one knee and kissed his ring, then stood and stepped away. I followed suit.

"I had wondered who it was that would invoke the code of secrecy, but now that I have seen you my blood grows cold. Brother Alexander," he said. "I received word of the Abbot and have sent strong objections to the treatment of one of us. An emissary from the Order is negotiating the Abbot's release, but the King's man is stalling our advances." He looked my way and greeted me. "Tormod MacLeod, if I remember correctly.

He turned his attention back to Alexander. "Brother, tell me what is it that brings you here so late in the year and at night?"

"Grand Master, we bring grave news. Several trainees to the Order have been seen meeting with agents o' the King. I fear that there are plots hatching an' growing within the Order," said Alexander.

The Grand Master met his eyes. "Have you names and know you what the meetings were about?"

"No, Grand Master, but Tormod would recognize them. He has seen their faces an' heard their voices," Alexander said.

"What do you propose?" he asked.

"Just that Tormod be allowed to join the ranks as apprentice, to follow an' listen to the conversations that are beyond our ears." The Templar was steadfast in his belief that I could do what we proposed. I was not as confident, for though I had seen them, I knew that at least one of them had seen me as well.

The Grand Master was quiet a moment, then met my eyes. "Is this something you want, Tormod? If what you say is true, this could very well be a dangerous undertaking."

"Aye, Grand Master, if there is aught to be done in the name o' the Order, I would consider it my duty to the Lord." I wished then that none of this had ever come to pass for a fear as deep and as wide as the great ocean washed over me. I knew that the outcome would have dire consequences for the Grand Master. In all of the visions that I had seen, this much was true.

"Then we will make it so. Cells have been readied for the both of you. Dinner has passed, but bread and cheese can be found in the kitchens. I warn you, watch yourselves. I have always felt safe and secure within the walls of our Order, but of late things have not been the same. I do not know of the trainees you speak of, and I have no powers beyond the strength of my hands, mind, and belief, but I feel a tension inside these walls that was never ours before." He laid his hands on my head. "Be safe, young man. Walk with the Lord."

And to Alexander he said, "You have been a friend

and ally for time without pause, Alexander. May the Lord's light shine upon you and whatever may come, let it protect you, always." He made the sign of the cross upon his forehead.

"Thank ye, my Lord Grand Master."

A QUESTION OF DUTY

Our cells were near to one another, on the second floor of the preceptory overlooking the courtyard, but when we bedded down for the night I was alone. Beyond my walls, men snored and slumbered as I struggled to breathe. The air was close and filled with the dust of the seldom-used space. Why was I here? Torquil was alone and fighting for life. My place was by his side.

I held the carving in my hands. It had been away from me too long, and I needed the feel of it not just in my sporran but also beneath my fingers. Since the moment Aine and I realized where it had come from I had wanted to study it anew. There was no light allowed in the rooms at night so I had to be content to learn the contours with only my fingers. More than anything I wanted to feel the shape of the face and to remember the image of Our

Lady, who had come to me in the visions. I brushed my fingers over the ridges of the wood, and suddenly, with a clarity that I had not encountered, I saw the trainees.

Huddled in a small room they whispered. *"I will give evidence first. Tell them of the secret rites of initiation. Blasphemy. Idolatry. Trampling on the cross . . ."*

"But that is untrue. All of it. You don't know what the rites of initiation are. We have not progressed to those levels. We cannot do this."

"We are in this. One and all. Promises have been made. You were ripe enough when the coin was paid."

"But that was long ago. None of this was explained. Don't you know what they will do to us? They'll burn us! For heretics!"

"We have been promised protection. Stick to the plan and we will have our share of all the land, ships, and property that the King will seize."

The vision broke suddenly, leaving me shaking and sweating in the small dark room, in what would some-day — perhaps very soon — no longer be the preceptory of the Templar Order.

REVELATION

"We must be prepared," I said, pacing the floor before the Grand Master and the Templar. Both sat in stunned silence as I revealed all that I had seen in this last and most illuminating vision. "I canno' know when this is going to take place, but God help me, I am sure that the time is not far away."

"We must begin the preparations," said the Templar. "No matter what comes o' this, the Order must be protected."

"I fear that it might be too late for that," the Grand Master said with a quiet that made me stop mid-stride as a breath of cold slid over me.

"What, my Lord Grand Master?" the Templar said breathlessly.

"Three trainees were missing from the Compline prayer last night. We thought perhaps that they were sick, but when we checked this morning we found their cells empty and their clothing gone."

"We must move quickly, then. What is most

important? What needs to be taken from here before anything else?" asked the Templar.

The Grand Master pulled himself from the darkness that had overtaken him. "We must move the libraries and the treasury. It has to be done quickly and somehow without drawing the notice of the King," he said. "A pilgrimage. We will go as poor monks in small groups, carrying what we can and loading the packs of donkeys. We will take the treasury and scrolls overland, along the path of Saint James, through the mountain trade passes, and into Berne. We must ensure that everything is moved beyond the borders of France, that the King cannot take it for any reason."

"But that will take a very long time," I said. "There will be many opportunities for the King to take it back."

"Not if we continue our lives as they have always been. All of our plans must be kept a secret. We do not know if there are more than the three involved in this. Only the upper ranks will know the whole of things. Knights will be enlightened only when they are required to be," said the Grand Master.

"Would it not be a good idea to move the ships as well?" asked the Templar.

"Gradually. The last will only leave when their plans have been further illuminated." The Grand Master sighed and made the sign of the cross. "May the Lord grant that all of our preparation be for naught."

"Amen to that," I said.

"Ye will take Torquil an' Aine back to Scotia on the next ship, Tormod."

We stood at a watchtower on the gate, staring down over the countryside toward the cathedral off in the distance. Snow was falling lightly, and my breath fanned out before me. The cold I felt now was far more than the weather. How could we know what would come of this?

"Ye've seen it, haven't ye?" We both knew to what I referred.

"Aye. I have seen him burn. I wish that I could erase the thought, but it follows me everywhere. I believe 'tis something that will not change." I believed still that everything I foresaw eventually would come to pass, but I did not bother to speak the thought aloud.

"I fear that day, Tormod." He appeared lost in a thought and for once I had no wish to know what it was. I did not want to think about anything that could frighten even him.

"Will ye come to us?" I asked, changing the path of our conversation.

"Aye. As soon as I am able. I want ye to retrieve the Holy Vessel when ye return. Take it far from the preceptory walls, Tormod. Ye have been chosen for a reason," he said.

I stared out into the distance, as if I could find that reason somewhere out there.

THE PATH TO ENLIGHTENMENT

"Is he strong enough to travel?" Aine asked, her hand plaiting the material of Torquil's tunic with worry.

"Between the two o' us, we should be able to keep him strong enough. The Templar ship will have healers waiting for us." I shared her fears.

"Tormod, what are ye thinking?" She stood and fetched a cloth that had been cooling by the window. "Ye've been quiet an' far off since ye returned."

"I feel that I have forgotten things that I should have remembered. The visions make sense now in the way they hadn't before. The carving was warning us that there was trouble in the Order. Since the ranks are swelled with gifted an' the new Protector had to be found, it would make sense that She would try to keep the Order from disaster. But is that the answer, the whole o' it?" I moved to the fire, trying to chase the cold that had settled in my bones. I feared sometimes that it would never truly go away.

"What more can there be, Tormod? I, for one, canno' wait to be rid o' these shores. The land here makes my blood itch." She sat again, gently washing Torquil's face.

"What about the seal? What about Gaston an' the parchment and red wax?" My heart dropped. "Gaston! Aine, where is Gaston?"

I raced from the room, calling for the footman and Fabienne and anyone else who might listen. It was Lisette who stumbled wide-eyed across my path. "Monsieur Tormod. He has gone to the castle."

They were the first words I had heard the little girl utter, and they brought the chill inside me to freezing. "Lisette, did he tell ye why he was going?" My voice was loud, and she dropped her head and hunched her shoulders as if trying to disappear. "Please, little one. It's important. What did he say?"

"He said that he needed proof, that the Templar Alexander would not believe him if he told." She stared up at me with eyes as innocent as an infant.

"Told what, Lisette?"

"I don't know, monsieur. Gaston talks a lot. He talks to himself more than to me. That was all I heard him say."

I took the swiftest horse I could find in Fabienne's stables and still I could not ride as fast as I needed to go. The road was painted with a thin and slippery coat of ice that churned beneath the horse's hooves and made moving quickly nearly impossible. It took twice the time to travel the distance from Fabienne's to the palace as it had just two days before and each footfall of my mount made my heart feel near to exploding.

A train of goods was making its way down the snaking path out of the main gates, and I had to slow and wait for it to pass. Following was the conclave of the Holy Father. Fourteen acolytes carried his litter, and row upon row of priest and bishop walked and rode beside and behind. It was within their ranks that I saw the Archbishop. And though I wanted to beg his help in finding Gaston, in his current position he was no help.

The wait was interminable, and I was nearly ready to climb over the last of them as they passed. But finally there was a space if, however, small to pass and I bolted through it. Thundering down the path I pulled up hard before the stables. "Take my mount, boy," I said to the stable hand, "I've urgent business within." I crossed the courtyard, hurried toward the kitchens, and burst inside. "Gaston. Where is he?"

Just then I heard a sharp cry from down the hallway, the shriek of a woman so frightened that the blood nearly drained from my body. I ran toward the sound at full speed, sliding around corners and pushing people out of the way. I found him there with the pool of his life's blood staining the flags crimson. "Gaston!" I cried.

I dropped to his side, cradling the back of his head where the gash had been made. It was a long cut, made by a sharp, curved blade, the kind that was not found on the common men who roamed these halls. He was already gone. The last breath had passed his lips while the Holy Father's conclave had held me up. It didn't seem fair. I felt along his tunic but found nothing stored beneath, but on his fingertips were the remnants of the cracked red wax on the parchment I now knew he had found in the King's chambers. Whoever had done this to him had taken whatever it was that he had found. I held him until the King's guard and healers gathered his body.

THE PAIN OF RESPONSIBILITY

I alone had the sad task of delivering Gaston's body to his mother. The feel of her pain was something I would not shield against. I felt responsible, as if I should have thought to find him sooner. I should have kept this fate from him. I should have known.

"Ye did nothing wrong. Not even Alexander foresaw this happening." Aine stood beside me in the dark outside the main house. I could not bring myself to be in the same house with Fabienne's pain. She needed space to grieve and, if nothing else, I would give that to her. The Templar had departed the preceptory at first light with the most important of the library and a good deal of the Templars' ready coin. With an escort of knights he moved with haste toward the borders. There was no way to reach him and let him know what had happened.

Torquil was awake and full of both pain and misery. Fabienne's house was not a place of joy, and I was not the only one who thought me responsible. It was strong in Fabienne's mind and a hairsbreadth from her lips.

"We should be on our way a' morning's light," said Aine. "We are not wanted here."

"I will see him laid to rest an' then we will go. He was my friend as he was yers."

It was a full day before the preparations had been made for Gaston's burial. Though the ground was frozen, Fabienne's servants had managed to clear a grave. In the waning light of late afternoon beneath a sky whose ominous dark clouds spoke of snow, we stood in a half circle as the priest from the nearby village spoke the prayers that would commit his soul to the kingdom of the Lord. I prayed along silently, filled with sadness. Huddled in upon herself throughout the ceremony, Fabienne acted as though we were not there at all. I approached after Gaston's body was lowered into the ground.

Fabienne was still and unyielding, her eyes the red of blood. I reached out to comfort her but she pulled away sharply. "If you had not come. If I had not given you succor, my son would be here today. Do not touch me."

It was as if a knife had been drawn along my throat. "My Lady, I am truly sorry for yer loss."

She turned away without a sound and reached for Lisette, who stood still and white beside her mistress. I was overcome by the grief that consumed them both. I felt as though I had been beaten.

In many ways I knew that I had.

WELCOME NO MORE

We left in the dark. Aine rode in the cart beside Torquil, who lay on his side in a bed of hay. I sat an old sway-backed mare that Fabienne's groom readied in the stables, pulling them through the rough, pitted roads to our destination. The trip had been the longer for it, and Torquil was in agony as the cart jounced and jarred his only partially healed body. I, for the most part, went over again everything that I could remember of Gaston's involvement.

I was no closer to the truth of who had killed the lad or why. What was he doing back at the castle when we had all quit the place, worried that Gaylen had gone to de Nogaret and that the King was about to have us all arrested and jailed any moment?

Though Gaston could have been attacked for his thieving, I was sure this was not the case, or perhaps not all of it, anyway. I saw again in my mind's eye the parchment with the wax seal on it. "Aine, join me in this," I said softly. Without more of a prompt her song swirled softly about my mind. I dropped my shields and she did as well, and we were immediately as one in the power.

The vision of Gaston grew sharper, and my eyes were drawn to the seal on the document. I knew the impression was the same as the lead in the library. The seal of the fisherman was on the document that Gaston had seen in the drawer of the King's writing desk.

What could it possibly mean?

The Templar ship was loaded and ready when we arrived at the shore. Food and water awaited us, as did a complement of knights from preceptories all over France who were headed to Scotia, where the King had no jurisdiction. The knights traveled in the clothes of the common fisherman to avoid the eyes of any who would be watching, but swords and knives were tucked in their clothing and all around the ship for easy access. Though we still did not know what was going to happen, the Grand Master was being careful and thorough in his care of the knights under his command.

The carving had been glowing with a sullen heat since I had raced from Fabienne's to find Gaston. My guts were tight with foreboding, though I knew not where the evil would strike. Worry for Alexander stretched within me.

Aine helped Torquil up from below and they met me at the rail, staring ahead into the blackness. "How fare ye, Quill?"

"A sight better than before, but 'tis hard." He sat atop a turned cask and looked off to the sails. He was hanging on tightly to his senses. His body was so frail and broken, my heart ached. Aine moved to his side and took his hand. I knew that she was the only one who could provide the comfort he would need to heal and I did not begrudge her attention to him, but I longed for her touch as well. Her eyes were strong on me. *I am here for ye,* she whispered into my mind.

I nodded. "I'm sorry that ye both were caught up in all o' this," I said softly. "I don't, for once, know what is to come, an' for that I am grateful."

Aine took my hand with her free one and closed my fingers in hers. Linked to Torquil on one side and me on the other, she softly began her song aloud. The ship slid out into the wash of the river and suddenly the power that swirled in the land, the sea, and the air rose up around the three of us. Torquil's eyes were closed, but Aine's were wide with wonder as the carving began to burn. Pinpricks of light danced over the dark decking.

The wind whipped and howled, tossing the ship and filling the sails.

The vision that overtook us was one that was shared. Where my sight was usually fragmented, and Aine's was always an echo, Torquil's had sound, emotion, and immediacy. Together we were granted a vision as complete as I had ever seen.

An army of soldiers moved in the predawn silence, their armor and swords softly clinking, the rush of their booted feet thudding in the night. The gate to the Paris preceptory was open and the men spread out, surrounding all entrances and exits. At the fore was Guillaume de Nogaret.

"Open up in the name of the King. By order of the Holy Father and King Philippe, the Order of the Knights Templar are hereby arrested for the charges of blasphemy, heresy, high treason, and unlawful acts against man. Surrender your weapons and come peacefully and you will live. Fight and you will die."

A handful of knights, servants, and workers were milling all over the grounds, pulled from their beds, bound, and herded like cattle into the courtyard. The Grand Master was the first to enter, calm, regal, and composed. *"Come peacefully, my brothers. We have done no wrong."*

De Nogaret advanced on him quickly and with the pommel of his sword struck the Grand Master against the side of his face. Blood poured from the wound but the Grand Master stood strong and silent in the face of the attack. *"It is over. You have lost and the King has won. All of your lands and your wealth will belong to the crown, and your precious Order will be disbanded in dishonor."*

"The Order of Poor Fellow-Soldiers of Christ will live on forever no matter what you do here today. You cannot silence God's servants." He lifted his hands and placed his wrists together to be bound.

De Nogaret was furious. *"We shall see about that. Take him. Take all of them."* He stalked to the gate. *"Load up the treasure."*

A soldier appeared at his side, his face white and slack. *"There is nothing here. The treasure is gone."*

"What! Look again!" he demanded.

"We have, my Lord Councillor. The vaults are empty."

The vision faded as the men, with the Grand Master in the fore, were led in ropes and chains out of the preceptory.

THE PATH LED HOME

The trip across the ocean was filled with many days and nights of shared visions. As Torquil joined with Aine and me, the power of the carving did much in healing the wounds of his body and soul.

From our linking, we learned that the King had demanded of the Holy Father an investigation of the Order. Templar preceptories all around the world had been surrounded at the same time and all within arrested, but because of the carving and the visions I had been granted, the Order had known enough in advance to get most of their men, all of their libraries, their treasure, and their ships moved off to distant lands and safety.

Some of the darkest visions were terrible to witness. We saw the Grand Master and a man of the upper ranks of the Order, who had elected to stay at their preceptories, tortured. Of the three trainees, two of them died in the prisons alongside the Templar dignitaries. The only one to survive was Zachariah, who disappeared before that fateful day and was never heard from again.

Scotia was a land riven with war when we arrived back home. Many of my brothers had gone off in support of Robert the Bruce, as had, I learned, a good portion of the Paris knights who had escaped. Torquil kept to himself most days, but when he wanted to talk I was there to listen and lend my support. Bridie had demanded they marry the moment he arrived back home, and she took the nursing of him back from Aine, who moved into our household as sister to my sibs and help to my mother with the new bairn, MaryAlice.

Two days past we had left the hut together, with the box that now held both pieces of the Holy Vessel. The cairn we had found up in the Highlands was just ahead on the slope, and Aine and I moved toward it anxiously.

"Are ye sure ye want to do this, Tormod? 'Tis a fair distance from home. What if ye should need it?" We stood on the crest of the hill outside the crumbled wall, looking toward the dark space of the doorway. Aine's hair had grown into its long and curly state once more and as she turned, it spread out on the wind, glistening with red and gold in the sunshine.

I turned to her and lifted my hand to cup her cheek. She kissed me softly. "We will know where 'tis if we need to find it. This is where it belongs."

She nodded and we moved past the low overhang across the courtyard and into the dark. The stairs to below held just as much terror for her as they had when last we were here, but holding hands we made our way to the bottom.

Carefully, I placed the wooden box on the hard stone table in the absolute dark that was the space. The odd humming like a swarm of bees played at the edge of my hearing, and Aine's breath seemed to pant in time with it. "It will be all right, Aine," I said, lifting the lid.

A spill of light, bright as the sun, filled the chamber as the carving began to glow. Aine gasped, and I turned to see what had caught her so.

In the illumination, we were able to see what we had not before. Every bit of the walls of the room were carved. In the center at the head of the table was the image of an enormous tree. The roots stretched around the whole of the room and its leafless limbs twined to the tops of the walls. In the space between were birds and beasts, some that we knew and others that we did not. On the ceiling were the images of clouds and sky.

In the middle of the table was a hollowed-out impression that seemed to have been worn by the touch of many hands. I ran my fingers along the edge and a great tingling sensation slid through them. Between the table and the ceiling was the odd space that Aine and I had felt before, blankness that was at once cold and strange.

"This is the feel that surrounded the land in France," Aine said. "'Tis as if in this place something is wrong. Something is sickly. Up here" — she lifted her hand toward the ceiling — "all is well. And down there" — she ran her hands along the table and beneath — "'tis fine. But between there is a hole. I think the two were at one time connected, but now they are apart an' the lower part is growing ill.

"When ye took the Holy Vessel from the cave, tell me what the space looked like," she said.

I thought back to the beginning. "Light radiated through the floor an' the walls an' ceiling as if the cave was connected to the Vessel," I said, remembering the wondrous place.

"An' have ye seen it since in any of yer visions?" she asked.

"Aye. 'Tis just a cave now. The light is gone," I said.

"That's it. That's why the land felt sickly. The Holy Vessel was bridging Heaven an' earth. When ye took it from that place, the bridge was destroyed." I stared at her with growing understanding.

"The visions I saw o' the land, sickly, with gnarled roots an' poison leaching — it was the breaking down between the two. I destroyed the connection." I was devastated by the thought.

"But perhaps it was all as it was meant to be, Tormod. Ye were meant to bring it here. To bring it home to the new resting place that had been prepared for it."

With shaking hands, I drew the pieces of the Holy Vessel from the wooden box. Aine placed her hands on mine and at once her song reverberated through the space. Together we united the two.

Brilliant color washed through the room. Light. Heat. Joy. Wonder. The power from below surged to meet the power from above, funneling through the carving to the bowl, through Aine and me. And in the space, a perfect harmony settled.

Together we released the Holy Vessel and turned to view the room in awe. The walls, the ceiling, the floor, the table, and the Holy Vessel glowed a crystalline white.

"This is where it belongs," I said.

"The bridge is once again complete," she agreed.

EPILOGUE

March 18, 1314

The carts rolled across the bridge and through the muddy streets as people shouted and jeered. Rotten fruit and vegetables pelted the ragged wooden slats and the men inside flinched beneath the onslaught. The crowd was thick with bodies pressed tightly together, their mood as high as if a festival and not an execution was about to take place.

Alexander, Aine, and I stood apart from one another, three points of the compass, north, south, and east. The platform with the scaffold was erected at the western point of the Île de la Cité, before the cathedral of Notre Dame. On the opposite shore, the King and his court crowded the parapets of the castle, watching to be sure at last that the Order of the Templar Knights was, without a shadow of doubt, finished.

The Grand Master, Jacques de Molay, and the Master Preceptor of Normandy, Geoffroi de Charney, were pulled from the carts by the ropes that bound their wrists. They were each a shadow of their former selves, withered and filthy, skeletal from years of torture, and a lack of food, water, and light, held as they had been in the dungeons of Chinon Castle deep below the city these last seven years. My heart ached for them. Nothing would change the outcome of this day. Nothing any of us could do would keep them from death, but we the gifted would join together today, perhaps one last time, to make their passing bearable.

I surveyed the crowd and saw many faces of the Templars who had gone to ground in the days before the dawn raid. They were alive and still practicing their faith in the Lord. Alexander and I had traveled the lands for many years seeking out the ones he knew to be gifted. We were, all of us, here out of respect and love.

The two men were dragged to the platform, tripping and stumbling without mercy from their captors. I wanted to press through the crowd and wrest them away, but held to my position even as I saw the blood on their wrists where the frayed ropes had cut and the way their legs shook as they staggered up the five steps to the top. Two lone stakes stood sentinel in the middle of the wooden stage. Tall heaps of kindling lined the platform's edge.

Aine's song began, outwardly silent, but ringing strong and sure within my mind. I called the power to me, reveling in the rush that set my blood afire. With a breath, I whispered over the gathered and I felt each of the gifted add to the net I was building and spreading. None of the non-gifted knew that anything was amiss.

I felt Alexander's strength as it added to my own. I was the main contact, the Chosen of Our Lady, and I would use Her Holy likeness, the carving, to accomplish what must be done. The Grand Master was dragged to the first stake. His soft words came to me as if on the wind. His request was to allow his hands be left unbound so that he could continue to pray. The executioner wavered, and I sent a strong command into his mind. *Ye will allow it. There is no harm in this.* The man moved on to the other captive without hesitation, leaving the Grand Master to his prayers.

I stilled my mind, calling on the triple grounding command, taking an inventory of the power available to me. There was more than enough to give peace to the men as they died and that was our main duty here.

As the inquisitor took the stage, the murmur of the crowd quieted and they waited expectantly. "Jacques de Molay. Geoffroi de Charney. You have been judged and found guilty by the law of the Kingdom. You have been sentenced to burn at the stake for your crimes. Have you anything to say?"

All of the gathered grew still and from across the water only the whisper of the wind seemed to cry in protest. The Grand Master raised his voice to the heavens. "The Templar Order is innocent. Let evil fall swiftly upon those who have falsely accused us. I condemn them to follow me unto death within the turn of the season." His eyes were focused on the King's palace in the distance as the wood was piled around his and de Charney's feet.

A murmur arose then, and the crowd slowly parted. Hope rose within me as the bright robes of the Archbishop Lambert progressed across the bridge. Slowly and regally he moved, commanding the eyes and ears of the onlookers. He passed by me not a hand span apart, and I held the power steady as I waited and watched with all of the others. Up the uneven stairway he strode and across the platform as the wood continued to be heaped.

Before the Preceptor of Normandy he stopped and slowly raised a hand to trace the sign of the cross. "Your sins have been forgiven. *In nomine Patris et Filii et Spiritus Sancti.* In the name of the Father, the Son, and the Holy Spirit. Be forever at peace." The whisper of de Charney was lost in the noise of the crowd. Then he advanced on the Grand Master, who asked him something that was lost in the riffle. The Archbishop made the sign of the cross, leaned in toward the Grand Master, and spoke several quiet words.

Unwittingly, I had begun to move closer, something compelling my interest. The feel of the carving, brought from the cave for the duty at hand, was alight in the sporran at my waist. I rested my hands on it and Aine's song rose swiftly in my mind as the collar of the Archbishop's robes parted and a small, golden ring suspended on a chain swung free.

Time seemed to stop. Breath seized within my chest as the visions crashed down upon me. The Archbishop bent over the bed of an old man, his hands clamped tight over lips that were trying to expel a dark fluid. The Archbishop removing the Fisherman's Ring from the dead old man, the Holy Father, the Pope. The Archbishop commanding Alexander to find what lay at the end of the map. The Archbishop meeting with de Nogaret, then the Templar trainee Zachariah, planting the seeds of the plan to destroy the Order. The Archbishop promising Gaylen the highest price if he would deliver the relic. The Archbishop commanding the torture of the Abbot that he give up the location of the carving. The Archbishop finding Gaston with the parchment sealed with the impression from the lead hidden in the Queen's library. The struggle that ended with a blade to Gaston's neck as the false orders from the Pope granting the King permission to arrest the Templars fell to the stone floor and into the boy's crimson blood.

And then there came more. Visions that I knew had not yet come to pass. The Archbishop being inaugurated as the next Pope. The Holy Vessel alight in his hands.

It had been him all along, the nameless, faceless evil that had been moving among us. We had all been unaware. We had all furthered his goals and not a one of us knew that we had been doing so.

Fury whipped suddenly within me and with a strong and violent push I sent the knowledge out to all of the gifted gathered. I felt the shock of the many and most strongly the Templar Alexander, whose roar of denial resounded within my mind.

And within that roar I remembered what he sought most to teach me, that the future could be changed. That I could bring about that change with my decisions and actions.

As the Archbishop stepped away from the Grand Master and started back toward the stairs, I sent my mind along a tendril of power straight into the paths of his body, winging through the blood, deep into his heart. And there I began to squeeze. As I had tried to make Bertrand's heart beat more strongly, I worked the Archbishop's organ in the opposite manner. I felt his steps begin to falter as he neared the stairs, and his eyes grew dark within his head. I watched his hands grasp his chest as he began to fall, and as the crowd parted in fear, I saw the chain snap beneath his groping fingers. As he toppled dead from the platform, the ring of the Holy Father disappeared beneath the scaffolding. Undisturbed by the unexpected drama, the executioner lay spark to the tinder beneath the last earthly leaders of the Templar Order.

Tormod, Alexander directed sharply in my mind, shaking me from the shock of what I'd done. Before me was the pained gaze of the Grand Master. Quickly, I applied myself to the task I had come for.

All of the Order used their gifts accordingly. Some drew all feel of pain from the men as the flames grew high and scorched their bodies. Some sent visions of loveliness into their minds, memories of childhood, loved ones, and beloved places. Some slowed the breath in their lungs and the beat of their hearts. And I funneled the pure and absolute love of the Mother directly into their minds. Then, with tears in my eyes, we commended their spirits unto the Lord.

We stayed until both had departed this world, until their earthly bodies had dissolved into ash. And then as one we prayed.

THE END

FACTS OF INTEREST

As (allegedly) prophesied by Grand Master Jacques de Molay, both the King and Pope who had orchestrated and allowed the extermination of the Templar Line died within the year.

April 20, 1314
Pope Clement V died less than a month after the execution of Jacques de Molay. It is rumored that, while his body was lying in state, it was burnt by lightning from an intense storm that rose up out of the night.

November 29, 1314
King Philippe le Bel of France died from complications that allegedly arose after falling from his horse while hunting.

AUTHOR'S NOTE

It was both difficult and gratifying to end this series of books. Difficult, in that there were so many wonderful threads and scenes to tie together, and gratifying because I have learned as much about history as I have of the craft of writing in the process. I hope you have enjoyed my efforts. I apologize for any errors that might have come across in writing about a time, not only so long past, but documented, at times, very scarcely. Remember that many of the characters are works of fiction, but do look up the history of the Knights Templar. In my research, I have been constantly intrigued and impressed by the Order.

ACKNOWLEDGMENTS

As always I thank my family, friends, and fans for their constant love, support, and encouragement. It's been a trying couple of years and I would not have made it without you. To my amazing editorial publishing team, Cassandra Pelham and Andrea Davis Pinkney, thank you for allowing me to follow this story through to the end with guidance, patience, and enthusiasm. You have my eternal gratitude. To my fabulous Speculative Fiction Group, most especially Lyndsay Calusine, who always manages to catch the small and incorrect details that would surely be my undoing, I offer all my thanks and love.

And to the angels who watch over me and mine (I include Templars in this list), you have my heart and soul.